ALPHA FIELD

GRACE HUDSON

ISBN-13: 978-1978125476
ISBN-10: 197812547X

Printed and bound by Createspace
DBA of On-Demand Publishing, LLC
www.createspace.com

Cover Design by Sanura Jayashan
Interior Formatting by GH Books

Sign up to the Grace Hudson newsletter:
www.gracehudson.net
Twitter: @gracehudsonau
Facebook: www.facebook.com/gracehudsonauthor
Goodreads: www.goodreads.com/gracehudson

This edition is also available in e-book
978-1-63587-292-7

To my partner.

1

The door to the weapons store cabin opened with a shudder, the light streaming through across Beth 259201's face. She looked up, wiping the sweat from her forehead and tucking a stray hair behind her ear. Her olive skin was darkened by the days of training in the sun and her arms had begun to fill out, the muscles defined under her tan tunic. She wore her dark brown hair in a plait, her usual messy locks secured out of the way as she leaned over the grindstone, spinning it with regular presses to the foot pedal. She held a piece of metal to the spinning wheel, sharpening the tip. Sparks flew from the edge of the stone where the tip made contact. Laid out before her were rows of crossbow bolts and the white ash shafts that would soon house them.

"201?" said Rafaella, her tall figure silhouetted in the doorway, her blonde plait curled over her shoulder. She wore a tan tunic fastened with a leather belt, her saber housed in its usual sheath. She made her way to the weapons table, examining 201's efforts. "Not bad, not bad at all," she said, turning the bolt tip in her palm.

"Raf," said 201. "You're here early."

"You're getting better at this." Rafaella fastened the tip to the wood. "Almost as good as Jotha."

"I don't know about that, but its better than my first efforts," said 201, taking her foot off the pedal.

She rolled her shoulder, feeling the muscles bunch and tense under her tunic. She ran her finger along the raised purple scar, its appearance rope-like and twisted.

"It looks better today, healing nicely," said Rafaella, lifting 201's sleeve. "You should get Cal or Lina to take another look, but it's not infected, that's the main thing."

201 pulled the sleeve back over her shoulder to cover the scar. "So you haven't told me why you're here."

Rafaella smiled, raising an eyebrow. She opened the door to the cabin, the sun streaming across the training field.

201 squinted, shielding her eyes against the brightness of the midday sun. Shouts and cheers echoed between the fields and cabins of the camp. She spotted Jotha, his hands waving in the air, holding some kind of drink in his hand. Adira ran between his legs, trailing a bright yellow scrap of material behind her.

The strange convergence of pitches resonated within 201, filling her senses.

Rafaella wandered past the weapons cabin entrance, tapping on an empty barrel.

"I needed you to help me with this," said Rafaella.

"Where's Cal?"

"She's gone to talk to Renn."

201's eyes widened. "Isn't he..."

"Dead? Yeah, she visits his grave to pay her respects. Especially now, at this time of year."

201 stared at her blankly.

"A grave. You know, a stone, carved with his name."

"You venerate a stone?"

"The stone is... it's a symbol. It's how we remember him."

"How strange..."

"Not really, not for us, anyway. So, are you going to help me with this or not?"

201 watched as Rafaella wandered into an adjoining cabin, emerging moments later with a new barrel. Its contents sloshed inside as she dragged it across the threshold. She pushed the barrel through the doorway, leaning on the edge as it righted itself. Rafaella blew a stray piece of hair from her eyes.

"You have no idea what's going on, do you?" 201 shook her head, eyeing the barrel with interest.

"This," she tapped the barrel, listening to the dull thud. "This here is, well I guess you could call it cider, but it's really spirits. It's made from cattail roots. And potatoes. Do you want some?"

201 nodded. Rafaella loosened the lever on the barrel, pouring out a tiny stream into a mug. She handed it over. 201 took a sip and scrunched up her nose. The liquid burned her throat and nose, the sharpness darting throughout her head.

"My eyes hurt." 201 blinked, eyes red and watering. Rafaella chuckled, pouring a little more in 201's mug.

"Then we did it right then. Come on, help me with this barrel. And don't drink that too fast." Rafaella clapped her on the back, taking hold of the barrel on one side, waiting patiently for 201 to pick up the other side.

201 and Rafaella rounded another cabin to find the training grounds transformed in various bright shades and an array of wildflowers adorning the cabins and tables. A strange sound filled 201's head, the jumble of tones familiar yet utterly foreign to her ears.

Jotha ran between Caltha and Bonni, waving his drink and cheering as they grinned at him, Bonni shaking her head and calling out to him as he retreated. Liam sat on a rock nearby, a serene grin on his face. A mug sat at his feet, tipped over in the grass. Ginnie, Lina and Symon chatted on a long, carved log, gesticulating wildly and chuckling to themselves. Kap, Vern and Petra stood near the middle of the training grounds, watching the proceedings with detached amusement. Former Vassal Beth 259292 chatted to the Epsilon Fighters Beth 259263 and Beth 259277, laughing and sipping cattail spirits.

A former Zeta Internee, Beth 259234 sat on a wooden bench, dressed in a bright tunic, her once emaciated features flushed with vitality. She held her little one, Beth 259301, bundled in an oversized tunic and a woolen hat. There was a pinkness to the little one's cheeks that wasn't there before. Little 301 watched the array of bright flowers and constant activity with wide eyes, a tiny grin emerging from her oversized cheeks. The former Zeta Internees were dotted throughout the training grounds, their arms slightly fuller, a semblance of vitality returning to their once hollow faces. 201 smiled at her new companions as she passed by, one hand hooked through the barrel handle, muscles straining.

"What is this? I mean, why do you do this?" 201 turned to look at Rafaella.

"It's our harvest celebration. All of us at the camp like to celebrate the beginning of the harvest. It is the time when we reap the grains, pick the fruits and drink the spirits we've made throughout the season."

"So, you venerate food?"

"Yeah, but it's more than that. It's a time for enjoying food, yes, but it's more about celebrating our ability to grow our own food, have a drink, enjoy the time and be with our friends." Rafaella grinned at her. "You know, fun."

201 scrunched up her face in confusion, glancing around at the food lining the tables, taking in the lively sounds and the smiling faces. She looked back at Rafaella, the hint of a smile on her lips.

"I'm not sure I fully understand it but I like it. This is a good idea."

"Yeah, we thought so. Come on, let's get some more barrels, they seem to be running low again."

After a few more trips to carry barrels and food, 201 leaned against a log, Rafaella perched close beside her, sipping from her mug.

Near the edge of the gathering, Caltha waved over at Rafaella and 201, Adira standing on a log, waving and jumping on the spot. 201 noticed the burlap targets beside them. They were adorned in bright outfits, with sticks resembling arms and bunches of wildflowers dangling from the ends. She reached out, stroking her fingers along the petals.

Adira pulled at 201's tunic. 201 looked down to find Adira's little hand holding out a plate to 201. "Look! Lina showed me how to make honey cake!"

"Oh... thank you, Adira," said 201.

Adira grinned, waiting for 201's reaction. 201 tasted the cake, the flavors overwhelming her senses. It tasted of the roses that grew by the main cabin, with a hint of sweetness, a sticky, pleasant sensation.

"Thank you. It's very nice."

Adira jumped on the spot, clearly pleased with her efforts. "I'll show you how to make it. It's easy," said Adira.

201 took another bite, nodding enthusiastically. "I'd like that," she mumbled.

"Ooh! It'll be so fun!" She grabbed 201's hand, leading her off towards a wooden table draped in cloth, filled with more strange and wonderful creations. "First, you get the flour. We grow it in fields, you've probably seen them out past the big waterfall. Then we have to grind it. Then come the eggs, we have chickens too, lots of them. Have you ever had eggs? Ma says you might not be used to them because you only had white squares for dinner, and lunch, and even breakfast!"

201 held back a smile, listening intently and following Adira's lead as she continued to instruct 201 on the intricacies of creating a honey cake. "Anyway, then you mix butter with the flour and add the eggs, and… and this is the best part… you add the rose petal water and bake it in the oven until it's done."

201 nodded mutely, searching the table for something else to eat. She settled on a small cake filled with a creamy mixture and topped with a layer of bright red fruit.

"Ooh, strawberries! I love strawberries," said Adira. "Ma says these ones are the best. Jotha bought strawberry seeds from a merchant in one of the townships. I wanted to go but none of us can go there, only Jotha. Anyway, we grow them in straw. That's how they get their name. Straw-berries!"

201 closed her eyes, marveling at the taste. Adira continued to chatter, but 201 had contented herself with sampling the array of food spread out before her.

"Anyway, when the cake is done, you get the honey syrup mixture. Did I tell you about that? I don't know, it's easy anyway, and then you pour the mixture over the cake and that's how you make honey cake!" Adira stopped to nab a strawberry topped creation, taking a bite.

"You're very clever. I'm not sure I can remember all that," said 201, catching Caltha's eye.

Caltha made her way to 201, an amused expression dancing on her features. "Is Adira wearing you out yet? She likes to talk. A lot."

"It's okay," said 201. "I like talking. Adira is very good at it."

Caltha chuckled, ruffling Adira's hair and sending her off to greet Lina, who arrived carrying yet more plates of food.

201 shook her head. "After that I feel like I know how to make honey cake, but I'm sure that actually doing it would be very different."

"Don't worry, I'm sure Adira will help, but she'll probably eat all the syrup before it gets to the cake. Here, this is for you." Caltha handed 201 another mug of cattail and potato spirits.

201 wrinkled her nose, taking a sip. The taste was bitter compared to the sweetness of the strawberries.

"Don't worry," said Caltha, laughing. "You'll get used to the taste. Maybe."

The celebrations continued late into the day. The sun had begun to nestle behind the twin cliffs, the air taking on a chill, despite the lack of a breeze. 201 seated herself next to Caltha on a long wooden log. Some of the logs had been arranged in a huge ring, surrounding the beginnings of the largest camp fire 201 had ever seen. Jotha and Rafaella busied themselves with the piles of wood, laying them in a complicated arrangement, the logs stacked highest in the middle. Rafaella scratched a dark stone against her knife, sparks falling on to a pile of moss. Adira sneaked up behind Rafaella and tried to blow on the moss, extinguishing it completely.

"Adira," said Rafaella, hooking her arm around Adira's shoulders. "You have to wait until the sparks take hold. And then blow gently. Here, watch me. And just stand back a bit, you're too close."

Adira stepped back and watched intently as Rafaella scratched the stone once more with her knife, watching the moss glow and crackle. She blew gently on the base of the moss, waiting as the glow intensified. She placed the moss underneath a pile of dry kindling, blowing patiently until it caught on the twigs, the flames snapping and crackling as the fire spread, weaving its way through the layers of wood.

The sun was fading now, a muted pink and orange hue spreading across the sky, tinging everyone's faces with a golden glow. The fire flickered, picking up intensity, still too new to radiate a powerful, steady heat. Large rocks surrounded the blazing fire, keeping the logs from falling out of place. Puffs of dirt drifted through the air as silhouettes moved from their logs, returning with food and mugs, the sounds of laughter rising up in waves.

201 could not fully comprehend the activities surrounding her but she appreciated the feelings she received. Adira ran around the fire, laughing and squealing as Caltha chased her, calling out a taunt that made Adira scream and run faster, her little face flushed and shining. A feeling of warmth settled around 201, much like the coverings that enveloped her when she tried to sleep. Though this feeling was different. She felt safe somehow, comfortable. It was an unfamiliar feeling to her, but one she hoped she would grow to appreciate more often.

A buzzing tone started up from 201's right. She

turned to find Kap holding a carved wooden object, strange, twine-like lines running from one end to the other, vibrating under Kap's fingers as he plucked them, one by one. The sound filled 201's head, awakening a warm, pleasant feeling within her being.

"It's music," whispered Rafaella.

201 nodded, tilting her head to the side, taking a sip of her cattail spirits. "I like it. It is a pleasing sound. At night in my quarters we had something like this, but it was dull, in fact it was irritating, especially when I was trying to sleep. But this... this is different, brighter somehow." 201 took another sip. "This tastes horrible when I drink it. I thought you said I'd get used to this."

Rafaella slapped 201 on the back, doubling over with laughter. "Don't worry, we're not used to it either. After a while you probably won't care about the taste. But drink it slowly, or you'll end up like Symon over there." Rafaella pointed, nodding her head. Symon's face was flushed, his blonde hair falling over his eyes.

"I heard that, Raf!" Symon stood, swaying slightly, stretching his arms wide, sparks from the fire surrounding his head as he cackled. Rafaella shook her head, turning back to 201.

"Like I said, drink it slowly."

"Raf?"

"Hmm?" Rafaella took a sip from her mug.

"What is that thing he's holding?" 201 pointed to Kap.

"It's a vihuela. You play it with your fingers."

201 turned her head to the sound of something that made her shiver. Caltha had begun to hum, then she opened her mouth to make a sound that fitted so perfectly with the vihuela that it was almost too much for 201 to bear. A tear escaped from 201's eye. Rafaella patted 201's shoulder gently, ducking her head. Her eyes were also damp, glistening in the firelight.

201 allowed the sounds, the music, she corrected herself, to wash over her. It was like something she had known before, a reminder of a feeling she had never had, yet knew like it was her own.

201 watched the flames as they danced over the animated faces of the former Zeta Circuit Internees. Laughing, talking, sipping on cattail spirits, eyes alive and finally seeing.

The flames dance before them, but this time the fire is under their command.

The soothing tones of Caltha's voice wound through 201's consciousness, brightening her senses and quieting the small voice that whispered within her mind.

But Zeta Circuit is never empty for long.

201 pushed the unwanted thoughts aside, bathing in the warmth of her new companions' laughter. She watched as Rafaella hummed along, occasionally joining in with Caltha and Kap, a shower of orange sparks from the flames twirling and winding up to the sky.

2

201 found herself swirling, trapped in a dream where cold stone walls surrounded her body, the small torch in her hand wavering in the airless facility, giving off an acrid smoke.

She felt along the wall, wishing for more light to guide her through the narrow hallway as the walls constricted with each step.

An Internee stood before her, blocking her path. She was dressed in the white jumpsuit of Beta Circuit.

"Come with me. I know the way out," said 201, her voice strange in her ears. She knew it was a lie. The hallway narrowed behind the Beta Internee to almost nothing. 201 almost felt as if the walls edged closer of their own accord. There would be no way out this time.

"No, traitor. I do not wish to leave. I have been promoted as Vassal, earning the veneration of FERTS. I will produce a Sire, the highest veneration..."

"No, you don't understand. You are not safe here. You will not be venerated. Come with me. There is no more time."

"Traitor," said the Beta Internee, smoothing her hair over her shoulder. "Officer! This Internee wishes to leave the provision and protection of FERTS."

An Officer appeared behind the Beta Internee. He smiled, grabbing 201's torch and backing away.

201's skin prickled as she heard the clunk of the iron lever. The remaining air sucked out of the hallway.

The fire rolled towards them, bouncing and weaving, climbing the walls and spreading across the roof.

The Beta Internee stared at 201, her eyes widening as the fire engulfed them both.

"But I don't understand. I am a Beta Internee. I am a Vassal..."

Her face dripped and blackened, charred lips peeling back to reveal strong, white teeth.

201 awoke to find a sliver of moonlight peeking through the window. She blinked, taking in her surroundings and waiting for the visions of FERTS to dissipate in the night air.

She recalled that Rafaella had put her in a spare room inside the main cabin, or to be more precise, she had half-carried 201 up the steps and removed her boots before 201 passed out. She remembered dancing, a strange set of movements she hoped to emulate one day, preferably without the hindrance of cattail spirits. She may have been humming the tune that Caltha was singing by the fire but she couldn't remember the details.

She sat up, rubbing her temples and waiting for the room to stop swirling. She watched the tree outside the window sway in the night breeze, its branches tapping against the window frame.

She couldn't remember why she had woken, but something had stirred her from her cattail spirit induced slumber. She rubbed her eyes, considering the idea of getting some air, despite the chill. She shuffled to the edge of the bed, pulling on her boots and stepping past the open fire, the embers too cool to make any difference to the temperature of the room. She stopped in the main room, listening for sounds of Rafaella, Caltha and Adira sleeping, hearing nothing of note.

201 paused at the front door, certain she had heard something outside. It sounded like a crack, or perhaps a crackle, she couldn't be sure.

"201?"

201 jumped, turning to find Rafaella standing behind her, fully dressed, holding a saber in one hand.

"What? Why do you have this?" she asked, gesturing to the weapon.

Rafaella sheathed her saber, fastening her boots. "Couldn't sleep. You too?"

"I don't know," said 201. "Something woke me, but now I can hear nothing. Perhaps the cattail spirits did not agree with me."

Rafaella chuckled, adjusting her belt and tunic. "Cattail spirits don't agree with anyone. Jotha insists on making it every year, and every year we complain about the taste. Still, it does the trick."

"Where's Cal?"

"I let her sleep. She keeps acting as if she's fine but I know she's not. She's too proud to admit that she needs rest, it's infuriating. She almost died, and she tries to carry on as usual..."

201 put her hand on Rafaella's forearm, tightening her grip. "Raf, something's not right."

Rafaella moved to the window, checking the camp for signs of movement. "Damn it," she whispered. "I can't see Jotha in the watch tower. I told him, slow down on the cattail spirits. He's probably sleeping it off."

"He's not asleep, Raf," said 201, grabbing a bastard sword from the collection near the door and fastening it to her belt.

"How do you know?"

"I just do. We have to move, quietly," said 201.

A crack sounded outside, the noise that 201 had thought she imagined. A chill went through her that had nothing to do with the coolness of the evening. Rafaella's eyes widened, then narrowed. "Come on 201. Time to move."

201 and Rafaella edged the door open, slipping through without allowing it to bang shut. They kept to the shadows, making their way to the watch tower. Jotha's familiar blonde head was absent from the top of the wooden railing. They kept their eyes trained for any shadows that didn't belong, seeing nothing out of the ordinary.

201 followed Rafaella, climbing the wooden rungs to the top of the watch tower. She paused, narrowly missing Rafaella's boot kicking out towards her face.

"Jotha!" Rafaella hissed. "Why won't he answer?"

Rafaella hoisted herself over the top rung, 201 scrambling closely behind.

"Damn it! Jotha..." Rafaella's voice cracked. Jotha lay in the corner of the watch tower, his tunic soaked with blood. His saber lay beside him, the tip bright red in the moonlight. His crossbow and bolts lay scattered across the wooden floor.

"I got him, Raf..." he whispered, eyes straining to open, then slipping closed. "Slowed him down."

"Shh, shh," said Rafaella. "I'm sending help, we'll get you out of here." Rafaella lifted the hem of his tunic, finding the wound. She hissed out a breath. "It's okay, you're okay, hold on. This the only place they got you?"

Jotha nodded.

"I'm getting Reno," said 201.

"Keep to the shadows and don't make any noise. We don't know how many of them are out here." She turned her attention back to Jotha. "Hold on, just... I'm getting Kap and Vern, they'll get you to Lina. She'll take care of you." Rafaella paused, her shoulders stiffening.

"What? What is it?" asked 201, peering over the top of the watch tower, trying to pinpoint the location of the intruders.

"Cal... Adira. Go, 201! Move. We need to secure the cabins!"

201 rushed down the ladder, pushing her bastard sword out of the way so as not to catch it on the rungs. She hit the ground, sprinting to the shadow of one of the cabins. She slipped between the wooden

structures, pushing open the door to find Reno on his back, his mouth partly open.

"Reno," she whispered. "Reno, wake up!"

"201?" His eyes flew open. 201 clamped a hand over his mouth to stop him speaking again.

"You need to be quiet, Reno. There are intruders in the camp. Jotha's been injured. I need your help."

Reno pushed aside the coverings, grabbing his tunic, fastening his boots and following 201 to the weapons store. She handed him a spatha, grabbing a crossbow and some bolts for herself.

201 squinted through the crack in the door. "Where are they? Why can't we see them?"

Reno moved past her, leading the way to a spot high on a hill near the adjoining training grounds.

They edged behind the rise, peering over the top.

"There," he said. 201 squinted, trying to make out shapes in the moonlight. Something caught her eye to the south west, a figure dressed all in black, the hood obscuring his face.

He crouched near one of the outer cabins, removing something from his cloak. 201 watched a spark fly up before she understood what she was seeing. She aimed her crossbow, squinting along the guide.

"Allow for the wind, 201, it's a north easterly."

"I know what I'm doing," she muttered, keeping the cloaked figure in her sights. She took a deep breath, held it, and fired. The bolt hit its mark, the figure collapsing against the side of the cabin. The sparks beside him caught and flames began to lick at the wooden beams.

"Bonni, Petra. They're still inside! Come on," said 201, pushing up and stepping over the rise.

"Wait, 201!" Reno grabbed her arm, pointing to a cabin near the entrance of the camp. The side flickered and smoldered and the flames were spreading quickly. Another figure headed for the surrounding trees. She aimed and fired, catching him in the leg. He staggered to the trees, blending into the shadows. She spotted Symon and Liam heading towards the tree line, sabers drawn.

A third figure limped from the back of one of the central cabins, clutching his midsection.

"There!" said Reno.

201 followed him with her crossbow, the dart shaking in her vision. "Jotha. That must be the one who attacked Jotha. Why won't he keep still?"

"Breathe, 201," said Reno, peering over the rise. "You can take him..."

A bolt pierced the hooded figure's back. 201 traced its origin to the top of the watch tower, catching sight of Rafaella's plait as she ducked underneath the protection of the wooden slats.

Another figure strode towards the base of the watch tower, carrying a flaming torch.

"Wait, that's not one of them..." said 201.

"Tor! You fool!" Reno charged from their concealed location, rushing at Officer Tor and knocking him to the ground. Officer Tor stabbed at Reno with a saber, catching him in the side. Reno knocked the saber from Tor's grip, clutching his side as he fell.

201 caught up to find them scuffling on the ground near the discarded saber. Reno cried out as Officer Tor's elbow connected with his cheek. Tor grappled with Reno, refusing to relinquish his torch.

201 glanced up at the watch tower. She knew that Jotha had not been moved, and Rafaella would be guarding him. The faces of Kap and Vern peered over the edge.

Officer Tor broke away from Reno, diving to the base of the wooden tower and setting the edge alight.

"Have you lost your mind?" yelled Reno, applying pressure to his side, the blood seeping between his fingers.

"My loyalty is to FERTS," he said, waving the torch in Reno's direction. "You consort with Internees? You are a traitor."

"Officer Tor... Tor, please. You don't need to do this. Just hand over the torch," said Reno.

201 heard voices and the sounds of water sloshing in buckets coming closer. She remained in position, crouched on the ground behind Reno. The flames caught, licking up the side of the watch tower. Rafaella aimed her crossbow down over the wooden railing, but the angle was too sharp for her to get the right trajectory.

"Get that fire out!" shouted Rafaella, motioning to Petra and Bonni, who headed for the tower with buckets of water.

Officer Tor bent to the ground, ignoring Reno's plea. He touched the torch to the next post, holding it steady. 201 slid the bone dagger from her boot, fingers pinching the tip. She flicked and released, the dagger spinning through the air and lodging in Officer Tor's chest. He crashed to the ground, the torch rolling from his grip.

Petra and Bonni arrived with the buckets, dousing the flames at the base of the tower.

"It's out, Raf!" shouted Bonni.

Rafaella's head peered over the railing, her plait swinging over her shoulder. "We've got Jotha up here. Help me get him down!"

Reno crawled beside Officer Tor, studying his face. "Why, Tor? We could have had this..."

"We send our gratitude to Pinn..." Tor's voice trailed off. His blank eyes stared up at Reno's face.

"Come on, Reno. We need to get you inside," said 201, holding out her hand. Reno took it, hoisting himself to his feet, his other hand wrapped around his wound. He pushed past 201, heading for the rear cabins.

"Wait, where are you going?" said 201, catching up with Reno. "You're hurt."

"I have to know," he said. He found the robed figure crumpled on the ground next to Bonni and Petra's cabin. The doused flames hissed from the blackened outer wall and steam rose in a plume. Another corner of the cabin still flickered, catching and licking up the side of the wall. He pulled back the hood, sucking in a breath.

"Do you recognize him?" asked 201. Petra arrived with another bucket of water, shouting out to Bonni as she splashed the corner of the cabin.

Reno shook his head, kneeling over the robed figure. The insignia beneath his robes marked him as an Officer of FERTS. "I'm a fool. I doubted you but you were right, 201. All this time you were right. I should have trusted you." He pushed himself to his feet but his knees buckled underneath him. 201 hooked an arm around his waist, supporting his weight as he walked.

"No more moving around, let's get you inside, come on." 201 led him to Lina's cabin, pushing him through the doorway, feeling a wave of heat from the fire.

Lina knelt before the hearth, stacking logs on top of the flames. She glanced up, tracking their movements as they staggered through the door. "Set him down there." She pointed to the heavy wooden table, brushing the ash from her hands on her tunic. "I'll go wash up."

201 arranged Reno on the table, removing his tunic. She touched the edge of his stomach, the muscles bunching under her fingers. The wound at his side was deep, bleeding steadily.

"Who was it, Reno? Did you know him?"

Reno winced, arranging himself to alleviate the pressure. "Yeah, I know him. Knew him, I should say. Officer Gatt. He was Epsilon Circuit. You were right," he muttered, running a hand over his eyes. "I should have known that the mercenaries were Officers of FERTS. It's the only explanation that makes sense."

"You didn't know. Nobody did."

"You knew," he said, squinting as Lina arrived with supplies, bathing his wound with a cloth soaked in clove extract.

"If you didn't believe me, then why..."

"Because I thought you might be..."

The door banged open and Kap, Vern, Rafaella, Bonni and Petra stumbled in, carrying Jotha's arms and legs, a stream of blood trailing behind them. Lina dropped the cloth, rushing to help.

They helped Reno to a wooden chair, arranging Jotha's limp body on the table.

Reno leaned back, his head lolling to the side. 201 allowed Reno to fall against her shoulder, watching the bustle of activity and listening to the sounds of boiling water and clattering emanating from the kitchen.

"Boil the needles! No, the bigger ones! Here, I'll do it!"

"Get the cloves. A stack of clean cloths. I'll get the string, soak it in the water first!"

"Damn it, what's taking this water so long! Why won't you boil?"

Jotha raised his head, his voice soft against the steady sound of blood dripping to the floor. "You get them, 201," he said, his voice croaking. "If I don't make it, get them for all of us."

"You're going to make it, Jotha," said 201, clenching her teeth. Reno groaned, falling against her shoulder again. "We'll get them together. Just hold on." 201 watched Lina and Rafaella set up the equipment on the table. Lina bathed his wound while Petra soaked up the excess liquid with a cloth. Rafaella handed Jotha a cup of cattail spirits which he drank in one gulp, his eyes watering.

"Do it," he said, clenching his jaw. Rafaella held the wound while Lina began to sew. Jotha let out a cry, his head falling back on the table.

"Well, well? What are we looking at?" Rafaella said.

Lina continued to sew, hands steady as she worked. "The blade missed his organs. It's deep but he's got a good chance." She held out her hand to Petra, grabbing the clove-soaked cloth and mopping up the edges of the wound. "Nearly there, just hold still, Jotha. You're done, Raf. Go on, out of the way."

Rafaella backed away from the table, pacing the room and clenching her fists. Her eyes fixed on Reno.

"You. You brought them here. You did this." She stalked towards Reno. 201 blocked her path.

"You are mistaken, Raf. Reno fought Officer Tor to save you and the others, including Jotha. He helped me to take out the intruders before they could burn the whole camp. Tor is to blame, the other Officers are to blame, but you will not blame Reno for this."

Reno slumped forward, his head resting on his knees. Rafaella edged around 201, palms raised. "I just want to talk to him, relax," she said, kneeling at Reno's level. 201 took a step back, huffing out a breath.

Rafaella lifted Reno's shoulders, pushing him back in the chair. "Get me the cloth and needle kit, 201," she said.

"Hey," she said to Reno, patting his face. Reno opened an eye, squinting at Rafaella.

"Raf?" he murmured.

"Yeah. We'll get you fixed up, don't worry." She took the cloth from 201, bathing Reno's side. His stomach muscles twitched under her hands.

Kap and Vern left to fetch some more water from the well and Lina left Jotha to rest, stoking the fire with an iron poker.

"Thanks Raf," he whispered.

"Is it true? You were trying to save us back there?"

"Yes. You would have been trapped. I didn't want them to hurt you."

Rafaella's face was somber but her eyes were amused. "Why not?" she asked, reaching for the needle and string. "Okay, this is going to hurt."

"Distract me or something," he said, gritting his teeth.

"We're out of cattail spirits." She glanced around the room. "Can you boil some water, 201?"

201 left to join Petra and Bonni in the kitchen.

Rafaella leaned forward, planting a kiss on Reno's lips. His eyes widened, then closed. She lingered for a moment, then pulled away, beginning to sew. Reno watched her movements, studying her features as she worked. He winced as she pulled the stitches together.

"There. Better?"

"You kissed me," he said.

"I know, did it help?"

"Did it help what?" asked 201, returning with another bowl of boiling water and some clean cloths.

"The stitches," said Rafaella. "You're all done."

"Thanks, Raf," said Reno, leaning back in his chair.

"You can put your tunic back on now," said Rafaella. "Or not." She smirked, heading for the door.

Jotha raised his head, chuckling as she rounded the table.

"Not a word from you," she said to Jotha, patting his shoulder as she passed. "You're supposed to be resting."

Lina returned from the fire, rinsing her hands in the clove solution and dabbing at Jotha's stitches. She blew out a breath, her white hair flicking out of her eyes and sticking to her temple.

201 looked from the Rafaella's departing figure in the doorway, then back to Reno. "What was that?"

Reno said nothing, the hint of a smile on his lips.

3

Rafaella gathered the group on the training ground, their numbers no longer small enough to fit in the main cabin. Two of the cabins stood out against the others, their blackened frames surrounded by ash.

"We're moving the plan forward," she said, gesturing to the map spread at her feet, secured with rocks to stop the edges curling up and flying away in the breeze. "We were going to wait until everyone was trained up but this changes things. They brought the fight to us, now we have to bring it back to them. It won't stop until we end this ourselves."

201 perched on a rock to one side of Rafaella. Caltha stood on the other side, peering down at the map.

"Is everyone clear so far?" A few nods and murmurs came from the assembled group.

"No," said 201, leaning forward on her elbows. "It's not going to work."

"What do you mean?" asked Rafaella.

"I have spoken to Reno, 263 and 277. They are in agreement with my thoughts on this. The only way to fight FERTS is from the inside."

"Have you lost your mind, 201?" said Rafaella. "You go back inside FERTS and you won't see daylight again. We stick to the plan and attack them." She pointed to a spot on the map. "Here."

"No," said 201. "They must believe that the camp is no longer a threat. Lina, Adira and 301 will be in danger. This is how it must be done."

"There must be another way," said Rafaella.

"It's the only way," said 201, rising to her feet. "The Zeta Internees cannot return, that is clear. I would not wish to put them in danger, regardless. 275 cannot return. Her back is injured. She needs time to heal." 201 turned to face 292. "And 292, it seems you cannot return with us, since you are known to have escaped and expired your Vendee. You would join the rest of Zeta Circuit, which would not help us, or you."

"But you escaped! You expired their Pinnacle Officer," said Petra. "What makes you think you can return?"

"No," said 201. "There is no evidence of my escape. They do not know it was me that expired Pinnacle Officer Wilcox." She grimaced at Petra, pushing away thoughts of that night. "It happened on the night you rescued Zeta Circuit. They think it was you," she said, gesturing to the group. "I am free to return to FERTS."

"Fine. You think they don't suspect you."

"I know."

"Okay, you know. But how does this fit with the plan?" asked Rafaella. "What is this, a suicide mission? You want to die in there? It won't help your fellow Internees for you to get yourself killed you know."

"I have no intention of being expired," said 201. "All I know is that I must return."

"But why?" said Petra.

"Because of what I see!" shouted 201, rising to her feet. "Some of us must return or it will not work! I cannot sleep soundly knowing that Reno, 263 and 277 are in there without me!"

"Okay, okay, calm down," said Rafaella. "And you. You're okay with all of this?" she asked Reno.

"We need her," said Reno.

"And what about..." She gestured to Reno's wound, now bandaged under his uniform. "Can you travel with that?"

Reno nodded. "I'm well enough, yes," he said. "What 201 says makes sense. Much as I'd like to stay, I mean, if that was okay with you, but there really isn't another option."

"Think about it," said 201, tapping a spot on the map. "You said this yourself. We can't blow up the beacon again, they will have rigged it somehow."

"Yes, we know that, 201, we'll work around it. We'll figure it out somehow," said Rafaella. "I don't like it when we change the plan." She looked over at Caltha, who shook her head, casting her eyes downward. Caltha knew the consequences of altering the plan at will, and Rafaella was unlikely to allow her to forget how close she had come to death when things had gone wrong.

"You know what I say makes sense, Raf. The only way to do this is from the inside. As far as our uniforms are concerned, Reno is still an Officer, I am still an Internee. 263 and 277 are still Epsilon Fighters. What if we return triumphant? The camp was destroyed, burned to the ground, they have no reason to think otherwise. The mission was a success. We return to veneration and take up positions within FERTS. The rest of the plan has not been altered."

Rafaella shook her head. "Why, 201? Just tell me why."

"The Internees within FERTS will not come willingly, except those from Zeta Circuit. They do not know what we know. It will take more than the arrival of an army to change their thinking. It will take more than force to change what they have been taught and what they believe to be true."

"This isn't going to work," muttered Jotha, adjusting his position to alleviate the strain on his stitches.

"No, wait. 201 could have something here," said Rafaella. "We can't just take them against their will, not if they believe that FERTS exists only to protect them." Rafaella shook her head. "Maybe they believe that only FERTS and its Officers can protect them from invaders, like us, for example. That's what we are to them. That's what they have been taught. 201 is right. First they have to understand, otherwise this won't work. If they don't want to escape, we can't force them." Murmurs of approval rose up from the group. "But you're right Jotha, I don't see how this is going to work."

"There are only four of you," said Caltha, casting her eyes over 201, Reno, 263 and 277. "The numbers are against you if something goes wrong,"

"Five," 201 corrected her. "We will add one more to our group, then we return to FERTS. The rest of the plan will be carried out as Raf explained earlier. Wish us luck."

"You'll need it," muttered Jotha.

201 narrowed her eyes at Jotha.

"Fine," said Jotha. "I hope you know what you're doing, 201. Good luck. I guess we'll see you on the other side."

"Be careful, all of you," said Rafaella. "Won't be much good otherwise. And anyway, we're just starting to like having you around." She glanced at Reno, then 201. "So stay alive, okay?"

201 smiled at Rafaella. "You too, Raf. All of you. I hope to see you again."

The group filed off from the training ground to make preparations, taking the map with them.

"201, wait." 201 turned to find Rafaella standing behind her.

"What is it, Raf?"

"There's something you're not saying, I can tell."

201 remained silent, her eyes shining with tears.

"Just tell me, 201. I can't pretend to understand what you went through in there, and... why are you returning? I don't get it. Just help me understand."

"Because I never left, Raf. Part of me, all of me, I do not know anymore. In here." She tapped her temple. "In here, when I sleep, I am still within those walls. I see their faces, Raf. They're screaming, always screaming." She wiped he eye with the sleeve of her tunic. "All I know is that I cannot rest until FERTS is no more."

Rafaella touched her shoulder. "I just want you to be sure of what you're doing. What you're doing is dangerous, to you and the mission. What you're talking about... it sounds like revenge."

201 shrugged off her hand, turning to leave. Rafaella grabbed her elbow, tightening her grip.

"201, we all want this. We all want them to pay for what they did to Dina, to Renn, to all of us."

"They will not be able to see what I see. Reno needs me there."

"That's not the only reason."

"No it's not."

"You're like me, 201, I know it can be difficult when you have an idea in your mind, but you don't know when to stop."

"I will stop when FERTS is no more," said 201, making her way to the charred outer cabin. She bent down, collecting the ashes in a metal tin, sealing the lid with her fist.

"What are you doing?"

"This is for me. To remind me. To remind *them*."

"Just be careful."

"I won't put the mission at risk, Raf," said 201.

"No, 201. That's not what I meant. Just take care of yourself, okay?"

201 gave her a smile. "I hope to see you again, Raf," she said, heading down the path to Reno, the cart, and their supplies.

4

Reno, 277, 263 and 201 arrived in the township of Stenholme just as the sun was rising over the surrounding hills. They passed the entrance to the township, marked by a pattern of scarred wooden posts and tree stumps. The remains of a tall metal silo stood out as a feature, rusted through in parts. Various animals dotted the fields, leading to basic wooden structures surrounding a large white building. 201 had imagined that the University would be larger but it was modest, almost clinical, its style similar to FERTS. Perhaps they had been built around the same time before the war, but 201 couldn't be sure. She wondered why this particular building still stood while others had fallen. It seemed to make no sense. Reno had mentioned that before the war, it was once a place of healing, just as FERTS had been, though its function had since changed from its original purpose.

The cart wound through the path, its contents gathering suspicious stares from the Resident Citizens. Reno pulled the horses to a halt at the entrance to the local market to ask one of the sellers for directions.

201 leaned forward, peering through the bars at the goods lined up in each of the stalls. She recognized potatoes, corn and a few other herbs that Lina had shown her back at the camp.

"What is that?" she asked the seller, pointing to a row of long, green vegetables. The seller shaded his eyes, looking through the bars to find who had spoken. He scoffed at her question, turning his attention back to Reno.

"Hey!" said 201.

263 nudged her in the ribs. "What, what is it?" 201 asked, turning to 263.

"They will not speak to you, 201. They speak to Resident Citizens and Officers only."

"Of course. I had forgotten," muttered 201, watching as two Resident Citizens brushed past the cart, looking inside for a moment, surveying the three Internees inside.

They were an unusual combination, two seasoned Epsilon Fighters and one dishevelled Omega Vassal. 263 sat on one side of the cage, her imposing frame resting on a wooden bench. She wore her red Epsilon jumpsuit, her messy blonde hair spilling over her shoulders. Though she was tired from the journey, her blue eyes were animated when she spoke. Her companion, 277, looked as if she needed some rest. Her light brown hair was matted and though she appeared formidable, she had lost a little of her muscle mass, the red jumpsuit hanging loosely around her shoulders. 201 was the smaller of the three, her 5'7" frame less muscular than her traveling companions, though her shoulders and arms had become more defined since commencing training at the camp. She looked strange for a Vassal, her olive skin darkened by the sun, catlike hazel eyes, one of which was still slightly bruised, though the marks were fading, and dark brown hair pulled back in a messy plait. Her Omega jumpsuit was worn and ragged, a large faded stain marring the front. She did not look much like a Vassal at all, but she did not yet have the appearance of a Fighter. The Resident Citizens appeared confused. The Resident Citizens generally expected to see a Vassal with manicured nails, sleek hair and impeccable grooming, not the scruffy sight they found before them. The Resident Citizens moved on, finding nothing to hold their interest.

201 chuckled, watching them leave. "I suppose we are not to their liking."

"You have never been to the townships, then?" asked 277.

201 toyed with her Vassal chain, twirling it in her fingers. "I was taken to Oaklance, with my fellow Vassals. I did not wish to be chosen by a Vendee."

"And were you chosen?" asked 263.

"No. I was not cooperative. I wished to fight them."

263 chuckled. "That is not standard Vassal behavior. If you looked as you do now, you would have made an unusual Vassal."

"I was never a Vassal," said 201. She watched the back of Officer Reno's bald head as he sat at the helm, clacking the reins and drawing them closer to a group of weathered wooden structures.

Reno left the cart at the entrance to a small but comfortable abode. There were a few shrubs outside and a small path leading to the door.

"So, explain to me what we're doing here?" asked 277.

"We need him," 201 replied. "He is educated and has technical expertise that could help us once we are inside. And he believes that Internees like us, women, can lead. We need his assistance. We do not have many allies."

"And it has nothing to do with anything else?" asked 263, raising an eyebrow.

"No, 263. I would not take us so far out of our journey for something as trivial as what you are suggesting."

"I suppose not, though from what I have heard, I can understand your interest," 263 said, watching the front of the abode for signs of activity. Another Resident Citizen strolled past the cart, tapping on the bars. 201 flinched, turning to stare at the Resident Citizen. He moved away from the bars, continuing on his way to the markets.

"Well, I hope he's as useful as you say he is," said 263. "What is taking them so long?"

Reno re-emerged, looking strangely out of place in his black uniform and leather breastplate, his bald head shining in the sun. His olive skin was darker, much the same as 201's, and he had lost some muscle, the angles in his face appearing more pronounced.

201 sat up straighter as she spotted the familiar figure of Titan following closely behind, carrying a collection of leather satchels. His blonde hair was messy, as if he had just woken up. In comparison to the usual somber Officer's uniform, Titan's dark blue tunic made him appear more relaxed. His eyes widened when he spotted 201 at the rear of the cart.

"201!" Titan rushed to the bars, peering inside.

"It's good to see you again, Titan," said 201. She reached out her hand to rest on his shoulder.

He paused for a moment, studying her face. "What happened to you?" He reached out to touch her face, pulling back at the last moment.

"Oh." 201 rubbed her jaw. The bruises were mostly faded, but she remembered that she had not seen a mirror for some time. "I was in a fight."

Titan glanced over at 263 and 277. "Did you do this?" he asked 263.

"No, Titan," said 201. "It was 299. She is... expired now. Look, it doesn't matter. You will come with us?"

Titan sighed, leaning on the bars. "You told me to stay away, now you tell me to come back. From what Reno has told me, you will be expired immediately if they find out what really happened."

"So... are you coming, Officer Titan, or did we come here for nothing?" asked 277.

"Yes, yes, I have told Reno I will return with you, but this is a foolish idea."

"Thank you, Titan," said 201.

"Well," said Reno. "It seems you all have much to talk about on the journey. We need to leave. 263, 277, you are coming with me to gather supplies. We leave before 12:00." He unlocked the cart, allowing 263 and 277 to stretch their legs.

Titan leaned closer to the bars. "I did not think I would see you again. What is this? Is this... blood?" he touched her Omega jumpsuit, the faded stain still visible.

201 lowered her voice. "Reno has not told you everything."

Titan shook his head. "Reno told me many things... but I need to hear it from you."

"The night I told you to leave FERTS, I expired Pinnacle Officer Wilcox. I escaped, Titan." She glanced around, watching for signs of any Resident Citizens. "Raf, Cal, the others from the camp, they saved the Internees of Zeta Circuit. But it wasn't enough. It won't be enough for any of us. Zeta Circuit will be empty for a time, but even now, more Internees are being sent inside. They can't wait, Titan." She lowered her voice to a whisper. "They will burn them, Titan, just as they did before. Just as they have always done. We need to stop them. You need to trust me."

Titan squeezed his eyes shut. He tried to speak but was unable to find the words.

"I do trust you, 201. But Pinnacle Officer Wilcox was greatly venerated here for all he has done. I know you must have had your reasons for doing what you did, but the Resident Citizens are unlikely to see it that way. He was the one who brought peace to the

Forkstream Territories. They believe in his ways, his vision."

"And what do you believe?"

"You know what I believe, 201. But I believe there is much that needs to be done to make others see what you have seen."

"I need you to help me, Titan. We need to make them see, all of them. Perhaps you need to see as well. When we return, you will understand."

"How did... I don't understand. They know. Officer Reno knows everything. Why are you not expired?" He gestured to the direction Reno and the Epsilon Fighters had taken.

"It was not this way in the beginning. I am unsure if I have his trust, even now. He believes something about me that I do not understand. But he knows enough to question what he once believed to be true and that is what is important."

Titan's brows creased in thought. "Perhaps he cares for you, but if he does, he hides it well."

201 chuckled to herself. "I'm sure he has reasons for what he is doing, but I doubt that is why he returns."

"Do you think... do you think he will choose you?"

"Reno does not choose Internees."

"That does not mean he will never do it. I hope you know what you are doing, 201."

Two Vendees dressed in fine clothing approached to the cart, addressing Titan. "She for sale?"

"She is not for sale, Wren," said Titan.

"I am not for sale," said 201, her words overlapping Titan's.

The other Vendee looked over at Titan, mouth falling open. "Why do you let the Internee speak? A Vassal does not behave in this way." He took a closer look at 201. "Though she is not much of a Vassal. I will wait for the next shipment. This one looks... damaged. Come, Wren, there will be others."

201 narrowed her eyes, tracking the Vendees' movements as they departed, her fingers caressing the bone dagger wedged in her boot.

"You weren't going to attack them, were you?"

"No, of course not." She leaned forward, peering through the bars and scanning the path. "It would have drawn too much attention to the cart."

Titan's eyes widened.

"They're taking too long. We need to leave now," she said. "If we don't, there will be questions, then there will be talk." 201 edged to the back of the cart to avoid the morning sun, the shadows of the bars falling across her face.

"Are you sure you want to do this?" asked Titan, unlocking the cart and filling it with his own satchel and supplies.

"Do you think I wanted to do this? I do not have a choice. I could have remained at the camp with Raf and Cal but I could never enjoy it, not until the others are free. I can't ignore it." She gripped Titan's arm. "The Zeta Internees, they are me, and I am them. I know what they risk every day, while I risk nothing. It will always be there."

"But you could be expired. So could the others... we might not make it out. We could leave now, together, 201. Reno would understand." Titan untangled himself from her grip, loading up the rest of the supplies and glancing around. "I have to lock this. It wouldn't look right if I didn't."

"This, all of this. You have just proved what I am saying," said 201, standing back from the bars to allow Titan to lock the cage. "The way people look at us, they don't see what I see. I see the essence, what is on the inside of you, the same as what is inside myself. But when they see you, they see an Officer, or a student, at the least a Resident Citizen. You saw it yourself. You know how things are. When they see me, they see a Vassal, or an Epsilon Fighter, or perhaps a common Internee. But I am none of these things, Titan. Perhaps one day, others will see this."

Titan locked the cart, hooking the keys to his belt. "I told you, 201. I have written many papers on the subject. None have been well received as yet."

They caught sight of Reno and the Epsilon Fighters returning with the rest of the supplies.

"No matter what I write, it seems they will not listen to me," said Titan, as he turned to make his way back down the path to assist Reno.

"Then we will find other ways to make them listen," whispered 201.

5

The cart made its way through seemingly endless plains, leaving the township of Stenholme behind them. 201 was glad to depart before the townspeople grew suspicious of their unexplained presence. It would do them no good to provoke talk within the townships, no matter how far from FERTS they happened to be. Of the Forkstream Territories, Stenholme was the greatest distance from FERTS in relation to the other townships, save for Fortmouth, a comparable distance to the north west.

Stenholme was many miles to the north east of the forbidden territories, referred to as such by the townspeople. No Resident Citizen was permitted to stray into the forbidden territories, as first decreed by Pinnacle Officer Wilcox.

201 knew it as the suspension zone, the sprawling desert surrounded by rocky, mountainous ranges, concealing the hidden location of FERTS itself. It was unusual for such a small number of Epsilon Fighters to arrive in any township without being sold to Vendees for private bouts and various other pursuits, depending on the Vendees' wishes. It was even more unusual for a lone Omega Vassal to accompany them,

especially one who was scarred and covered in suspicious stains that refused to budge, no matter how many times 201 had washed her jumpsuit since her departure from FERTS. Still, the visit had passed without incident, as far as they could tell, and they had one more addition to their small but determined group.

201 reached through the bars and tapped Titan on the shoulder. He jumped, adjusting his grip on the reins at the helm of the cart.

"What is it, 201?" he asked.

"This." She handed through a scrap of paper, the symbol crudely drawn in charcoal. The line swirled from the outside to the inside, coming to a singular point. "Have you seen this? What does it mean?"

Titan handed the reins to Reno, unfolding the paper. He studied it for a moment, folding it and handing it back to 201. "Did you draw this?" 201 nodded. "Hm, I haven't seen this one. It was not part of our studies, but the books are there, if you care to find them. I cannot remember the name of the books, but I know that symbols such as these were widely used to create meaning and commune with nature. This one... it's a spiral. I believe it may have been used by the women, the wise ones, many years before the war."

"Tell me," said 201, leaning against the wooden bars. "What is the meaning of a symbol such as this? This spiral, as you call it. Did they venerate it? What was its purpose?"

Titan pondered the question, taking the reins from Reno and clacking the leather to speed their progress. "I do not think so. No, symbols such as these were not used for veneration. It wasn't like that. The symbols were secondary to the joining of energies. A symbol like that one, it would have been something that they would have used to focus their energies, draw their spirits together to increase their powers."

"You mean their essence?"

"I suppose you could call it that."

"And what did it do?"

"That's all I know, 201. What I have read is merely speculation. There are few remaining books on the subjects and like I said, they are not widely studied. FERTS has influenced our studies in many ways. The older books, they are mostly forgotten. They are not forbidden, as little is known of their existence, but such things are not encouraged, as you can imagine."

The cart bumped along rough ground, the dry, clumped earth giving way to smooth fields, wild crops bending and twisting in the breeze.

"Where did you see it?" asked Titan, turning the horses towards the first sighting of the Elan river. Reeds bracketed the forked streams of running water, merging together to form a large waterway that flowed towards the south.

"It was a carving. I saw it on a cave wall, on the way to the camp. I could not tell how long it had been there, but now I can't stop thinking about it." 201 turned to watch the back of Reno and Titan's heads at the helm of the cart. "So what you mean is that the symbol was secondary to the energies of the wise ones? That perhaps the symbol alone is not important?"

"I cannot answer that, 201," said Titan. "This symbol would not been used for many, many years. Much of the knowledge of the wise ones has been lost in time. The wise ones are no more, their ways are forgotten. The war, the dark times, the creation of FERTS, you know the rest. I suppose things were very different before our time."

"I just hoped... I hoped it would help somehow. I thought *you* could help. Perhaps I was wrong."

"You are like them, 201," said Titan. "I am sure of it. If anyone can use it to help us, I would expect it would be you."

201 leaned against the wooden bench, considering Titan's words. She watched through the bars as the cart bounced and jolted past stretches of fields interspersed with trees that soon transformed into thick forests. The cart drew closer to the river. 201 watched the sun sparkling over the surface of the water, creating patterns in the ripples that swirled together before breaking apart, as if they were never there at all.

6

Reno took the reins for the last stage of the journey. The suspension zone stretched for miles in all directions, the distant mountains overlooking the rocky desert. Stones flew from underneath the wheels as they passed green and purple shrubs and strange desert plants. They had used much of the remaining water and the welcome sight of the Elan river was now behind them. 201 clutched her knees, squeezing her eyes shut.

This was a mistake.

The closer the cart drew to FERTS, the more she was aware of her mind's activity spiking, images flickering before her eyes. Pinnacle Officer Wilcox's presence grew stronger with each turn of the cart's wheels and 201 found herself pushing against his cloying influence, struggling to clear her mind.

"What is it, 201?" asked 277, touching her arm.

"Nothing, nothing," said 201, shrugging her off. "I just... I'm not looking forward to returning."

"None of us are looking forward to it," said 263, watching through the bars as the cart traversed through mountainous terrain, skidding on pebbles as they climbed. "We must all be senseless to even consider this."

"We're not doing this for us. We're doing it for them." She pointed towards the end of the suspension zone, the larger stones giving way to pebbles, transforming into the smooth grasses of FERTS. "We must appear pleased to return," said 201. "We are expected to feel triumph at our achievements, and we must act accordingly, no matter how we feel." 201 attempted a smile.

"You do not look triumphant, 201," said 277.

201 took a deep breath, remembering her Vassal training. She smiled her presentation smile, imagining she was back at the camp, far from the suspension zone, listening to the sounds of the vihuela music and surrounded by the laughter of her companions as she watched the fires at night.

"That's better," said 263. "We can do this."

"Yes," said 201. "I know we can. It's just... I am afraid, I know we all are. But we cannot show how we feel, not to our fellow Internees, and especially not to the Officers. There is much that depends on what we do. We all know what needs to be done. Now we get to find out if it will work."

The cart bounced along the trail, nearing the edge of the suspension zone. The tips of the tree line came into view. 201 spotted the safe marker, denoting the last place where they would be free from the influence of FERTS.

"This is it. No turning back now," she muttered. She saw 263's knuckles whiten, clutching the wooden bench. 277 sat upright, the tightness of her jaw the only indication of her apprehension.

201 gripped the bars of the cage as FERTS came into view. The large stone building looked out of place here amongst the rocky desert and grasses bracketed by thick forest.

She shivered, the images of what lay beyond the far tree line hovering in her thoughts. She released the bars, digging her fingernails into her palms, willing the images to disappear.

Titan turned in his seat to peer at 201 through the bars. "How are you doing?"

"How do you think I am doing?" she said. "I must be out of my mind," she muttered, turning to stare at the view from the bars.

"Why does nobody ask how we are doing?" 263 said, a smirk on her face.

"I will ask then," said 201. "How do you feel about returning to FERTS?"

263 looked over at 277, shaking her head. "We are foolish to return here. Nothing good will come of this."

"We have to believe we are doing the right thing, 263, or we will lose our senses," said 201, forcing a smile. "Are you ready to do your duty for FERTS?" she said through gritted teeth.

263 and 277 smiled, bowing their heads. "We are ready to do our duty for FERTS," they said in unison.

"Quiet!" said Reno. "We're almost there."

277 stiffened. "Why is the Pinnacle Officer here?" she whispered.

201 spotted Pinnacle Officer Cerberus at the entrance, flanked by two guard Officers, his silver uniform and insignia gleaming in the sunlight.

"Keep smiling, 277," muttered 201. "Just keep smiling."

"Officer Reno returns!" said Pinnacle Officer Cerberus, stepping towards the cart to greet Reno. "And Officer Titan, you have decided to return to us?"

Titan cleared his throat. "Yes... Pinnacle Officer. My father has deemed it suitable for me to return. He no longer requires my assistance."

"Excellent, young Titan. This is excellent news. Give my regards to your father next time you see him." He turned his attention back to Reno. "Now, Officer Reno. What of your success against the rogues? You must tell me news of your achievements." He peered through the bars. "Oh, but what is this? An Omega Vassal amongst our brave Epsilon Fighters? I trust this will be an interesting story."

"She is also a brave defender of FERTS, Sir." Reno tapped the bars near 201's head, causing her to flinch. "She was captured by the rogues and managed to fight her way out of their clutches. She was also pivotal in taking down the camp. The camp is no more, Sir. Only ashes and cinder. The journey was indeed a success. All involved deserve veneration, subject to your approval of course."

Pinnacle Officer Cerberus stared at 201, nodding at Reno's words. "Excellent. Yes, of course, of course. You have made FERTS proud, dear Epsilon Fighters and... Vassal. Come, Reno, let us dine and speak of your travels. I'm sure you have much to tell me." Reno departed, following Pinnacle Officer Cerberus through the entrance at FERTS. Titan alighted from the helm, unlocking the bars.

"Don't draw attention to yourselves," he whispered. "Just look proud or triumphant or something." 201 continued smiling, though she was sure it was beginning to fade. "Try to look pleased," he said, nudging 201. "You will give us away before we can even get inside."

"Yes, Officer Titan," said 201. "We shall follow you. We are proud of our service to FERTS and take great delight in our duties." 263 smiled at 277, who mirrored her expression. 201 looked away from her companions, her nerves overtaking her composure. She ignored the improper urge to laugh, for fear that once she started, she would never stop.

"Come on, all of you," said Titan, pushing them through the entrance and towards Epsilon Circuit. "You look pleased enough. Follow me."

"We will truly be pleased when it is over," whispered 201, making her way past 263 and 277, heading for her newly assigned quarters at Epsilon Circuit.

GRACE HUDSON

7

Pinnacle Officer Cerberus settled himself behind his desk, toying with a quartz paperweight. Reno's food lay untouched on the plate before him. He took a small bite, not wishing to appear ungrateful in the presence of the Pinnacle Officer.

"So, Officer Reno," said Pinnacle Officer Cerberus, pushing away his plate and wiping his mouth. You sustained many casualties, that much is clear. Was the plan carried out as specified?"

"Yes, Sir. The plan was carried out according to your specifications. Nothing of the camp remains, only ash."

"Well, then, Reno, I believe we can deem this expedition a success."

"A success?" said Reno, resisting the inappropriate urge to shout at his superior.

Pinnacle Officer Cerberus tilted his head, a hint of a smile at his lips. His smile did not reach his eyes.

Reno shook his head. "Sir, all of the Zeta Internees were expired. Officer Tor, 299, I lost many of my best Fighters in the battle."

Pinnacle Officer Cerberus continued to study Reno, his smile growing stale.

"But you are correct, Sir, the mission was a success. The rogues were conquered as per your orders. In fact, a fire broke out at the camp. It is the very reason I am here today, along with my remaining Fighters. The rest were lost in the blaze. We were able to salvage the cart and the horses. There was no time for anything else."

The Pinnacle Officer pursed his lips. "So the fire... assisted your escape?"

"That is correct. The mercenaries that invaded the camp did not survive. The fire was fortunate for myself and my Fighters, however the camp's rogues were not so fortunate," said Reno.

Pinnacle Officer Cerberus hummed to himself, toying with his paperweight. Reno watched him, brows creased.

"Why do you look so serious, Reno? We had no use for the Zeta Internees, that is of no consequence to us. Zeta are a drain on the facility and resources. Though I still wonder what these rogues thought they were doing? Of course, we can all understand the desire to steal a Vassal, or indeed many Vassals. Vassals from Beta Circuit, Omega Circuit, these all have intrinsic value. Even an Epsilon Fighter, though far less attractive than a Vassal, of course, even they would fetch a much better price. But what value is a Zeta Internee to them? Why would they steal only Zeta Internees? It makes little sense to me. They would barely receive a sack of grain for the entire Circuit."

Reno kept his expression neutral. "From what I understand of these rogues, Sir, they were not very bright. They seemed to have no understanding of value, no logic to their actions."

"Clearly not. They could not have the wisdom and understanding we enjoy here at FERTS. I suppose they know only chaos, so different to our fine model of order and stability here. The great Pinnacle Officer Wilcox brought peace to the Forkstream Territories, and what do these rogues bring?" He paused, scratching his chin. "Chaos. They bring war and chaos. And I suppose, being not very bright, as you put it, I suppose at the very least they could fight, am I correct in assuming this?"

"Yes, they could indeed fight." Reno fixed his gaze on the quartz paperweight, watching it as it caught the light. "Some of the rogues appeared to have a rudimentary grasp of combat, but they were no match for the trained Fighters of Epsilon. Our Fighters have precision, discipline..."

Pinnacle Officer Cerberus leaned forward, studying Reno's face. "I thought you said the fire aided your escape, not your Fighters' skill."

"Initially they had the numbers, that is correct. But we were only temporarily confined. It's true they held the advantage for a time, but the skill of our Fighters conquered the rogues, as is to be expected. We merely waited for the right time."

"Of course, of course."

A silence descended, drawing out a little more than was comfortable for either of them.

Pinnacle Officer Cerberus watched Reno, his hands folded underneath his chin. "And what of the Omega Internee? She intrigues me, Reno. Where does she fit in to all of this?"

"She was taken by the rogues, though she managed to escape. We found her and returned her to the safety of the cart. As you can imagine, she was relieved to be once again under the protection of FERTS. In the battles that followed, she turned out to be a worthy addition to our efforts against the rogues in the camp."

"Hmm." Pinnacle Officer Cerberus put his finger on top of the paperweight, tapping the quartz. "She will be stripped of Vassal status and returned to Epsilon, then. I would presume this new addition would be beneficial to the Circuit?"

"That was my thinking, yes." Reno stood to leave, smoothing his rumpled uniform. He watched as the dust from his clothing drifted through the air, settling around his feet.

"So... you did not speak with the mercenaries that set light to the camp?"

Reno paused in the doorway. "No, Sir. They fought against the rogues, perhaps they were rivals, I do not know. They were not as fortunate as myself and the remaining Fighters."

"A pity..." he mused, leaning back on his chair. "I would have liked to find out more about them."

Reno nodded, hovering in the doorway.

"You are dismissed, Officer Reno. You may go now and resume your duties at Epsilon Circuit. I expect your full report on my desk in the morning."

"Thank you, Sir." Reno passed the stoic guard Officers further down the hall, acknowledging them with a quick nod of his head. A chill settled over him as he walked down the hallway that had nothing to do with the temperature.

I never told him that it was the mercenaries who set fire to the camp.

201 sat on one of the long rows of benches, wedged between two unfamiliar Epsilon Fighters. The ration room bustled with activity, the clatter of metal trays filling the air.

The excitement was palpable. She could sense the weight of curious eyes upon her but kept her head down, studying her squares of regulation protein with a detached fascination. She watched 263 and 277 from the corner of her eye, careful not to draw attention to herself. The two Epsilon Fighters were surrounded by well-wishers, celebrating their shared victory against the rogue camp. Occasionally, a snippet of conversation drifted across the hall, making its way to 201's ears.

"Veneration..."

"Defenders of FERTS..."

"Thankful for your return..."

201 took a bite of her regulation protein. During her time at the camp, she had tried to forget the texture of the bland, tasteless squares. The first bite reminded her of the very reason why she had suppressed the memory. She wrinkled her nose, ignoring the taste, or lack thereof.

The Epsilon Internee on her right leaned closer, her black hair swinging over her shoulder, forming a curtain between 201 and the other Internees. "You were with Reno's party of Fighters?"

201 nodded, forcing herself to swallow her rations.

"Then why are you not with 263 and 277?" She lowered her voice, giving the group a sideways glance. "It seems they are taking all the adulation without you."

201 shrugged. "I do not care for it."

"How strange." She reached out her hand. "I am Beth 259254."

"Beth 259201." 201 smiled, shaking her hand, doing her best to appear amiable.

"I have heard many things about you."

"Oh." 201 took another bite. "I will understand if you do not wish to be seen with me."

"It's not that, I do not mind being seen in your company. But it seems to me that you behave in strange ways."

201 nodded, squinting as she swallowed her regulation protein. "I suppose to some, my actions appear strange. I do not think I am particularly unusual," said 201.

"Don't worry, I do not believe most of what I hear. Us Epsilon Internees enjoy our speculation. I suppose it helps to keep our interest in between Fighter selection and the Epsilon Games. But you must be an effective Fighter if you joined Reno's party as a mere Vassal. Vassals do not fight, not the ones I have seen anyway."

"I am not a Vassal." 201 shook her head, feeling the absence of her Vassal chain around her neck.

"Well of course not, now that you have been transferred to Epsilon Circuit. Or demoted, I suppose it depends on how you look at it. What is your chosen weapon?"

"Bastard sword."

"Mine is trident. If you are chosen as Fighter, I will wish you good fortune."

Later that evening, 201 lay in her quarters at Epsilon. She stared at the ceiling, listening to the sounds of piped music filtering through the room. The door to her bathroom was ajar, allowing a glimpse of the now familiar fixtures. If she closed her eyes, she could imagine she was back in her old quarters at Beta, or Epsilon, or even Omega. A door was slightly to the left or right, perhaps offset or facing the other way, but they were all the same. Only her jumpsuit had changed this time, the blue of Omega replaced by the red of Epsilon Circuit.

201 stared through the slivered window to her right, a single beam moonlight breaking through across her pillow. When she thought about it, she had been an Internee at three of the five Circuits at FERTS, if indeed you could categorize Zeta as a Circuit. She resolved to be more careful about observing regulation at all times, in order to avoid the risk of transfer. She hoped she would not do anything that would cause her to be sent to Kappa, where she would chop wood all day until she collapsed from exhaustion, in which case she would then be

transferred to Zeta. But to be an Internee in three Circuits? Surely that was unusual. She wondered if she was the only one to have done this, and whether it was worthy of significance. She supposed it didn't matter, just as it didn't matter when she was demoted from Beta Circuit for breaking muscle mass regulations.

She did not miss the Vassal training, the countless nights of half-rations, the endless bathing, polishing and manicuring. Her only solace was the absence of a Vassal seduction technique manual beside her bed, with its crude drawings and its multitude of behavioral guides. She had been unable to master its requirements when undergoing Vassal training and did not expect her technique had improved since then.

She did not relish the idea of being put up for Fighter selection either, but Reno had given her his word, which she accepted as a guarantee. It was a promise of his commitment to their shared goal. She would be protected from the draw of Fighter selection, and subsequently spared from the random selections of the Epsilon Chance Wheel.

201 fell asleep listening to the rapid pulse of her heartbeat. She breathed shallowly, skimming the edges of sleep.

201 dreamed of a voice, the voice she now knew as the voice of Pinnacle Officer Cerberus, reverberating through her mind.

"Just a simple electronic device really, quite basic. The perimeter is small, just past the edge of the suspension zone. The siren emits a radio frequency wave, which of course can be set to expire the Internee with an electrical charge should they try to escape. But the beauty, the ingenuity of my new addition is this, when I sound the siren, or our modified device here, the frequency of just around 450MHz will produce what I'm sure you will agree is a startling result."

Cerberus' voice droned on, speaking of frequencies and percentages and various other details that made no sense to 201. She gripped the sheets, a trickle of sweat making its way from her temple to her pillow.

The voice of Beth #1 joined the incessant drone, speaking over the Pinnacle Officer, but 201 could not make out the words. The only word she could decipher from the overlapping voices was a familiar one.

Shield.

A strange image, the image of what could be deemed a shield rotated before her, showing markings of the symbol, a spiral adorning its face. But this was not like any shield 201 had encountered before at the Epsilon Games or in the weapons store room. It was thin, made from some kind of metal that gleamed pink in one light, orange in another. It bent and twisted before her, wrapping around itself and splitting apart into a coil, unwrapping and stretching out in her vision.

She woke to the sound of piped music, her heart beating too fast and her pulse throbbing inside her ears. She shuddered, hissing out a breath. 201 settled back into the soft coverings, allowing the music to draw her back into a shallow sleep.

9

The following morning, 201 stared ahead, her shoulders aligned with her fellow Epsilon Internees. They stood, spaced at arms length apart, standing in regulation order.

What am I doing here? Have I lost my senses?

The Officer stood at the railing, eyes bright with fervor, calling out the FERTS Requital. "Internees of Epsilon. We are gathered here to send our gratitude to Pinnacle Officer Cerberus and FERTS, for our daily provision and protection from those who would strike against our Vassals, our Fighters and our Internees."

"We send our gratitude to Pinnacle Officer Cerberus and FERTS," came the reply. 201 mouthed the words, or at least some of the words. She may have changed the words a little, but who was to know? It was her only way to distract herself in her unfortunate but self-imposed predicament. She studied the faces of her fellow Internees, watching as their eyes brightened at the mention of their beloved Pinnacle Officer.

"All Internees report to ration room before training commencement."

She caught up with 277 and 263 who walked with their shoulders almost touching, heads bent in private conversation. 201 touched 277's arm, stopping their progress on their way to the rations room.

"Have you had any luck so far?" she whispered to 277, glancing over at 263. 277 shuffled to the side, allowing the rest of the Epsilon Internees to pass through on their way to the ration room.

"We cannot speak for long, 201. We cannot do without rations this morning. We have muscle mass that we wish to regain. Be quick." 277 glanced at the familiar faces in the crowd, waving to her fellow Epsilon Fighters.

"Why?" asked 201, looking them over. She lowered her voice, making sure that there were no Internees close enough to hear. "You do not need to prepare for the Epsilon Games. Reno has given his word that none of us will be chosen."

"We do not do this for the Epsilon Games, 201. We are in preparation for... the plan," she whispered. "We will need our strength."

"I will not keep you, then. I know you do not wish to be seen in my company, but did you make any progress at evening rations? What did they say?" said 201, ignoring the passing line of Epsilon Fighters, who in turn ignored her.

277 turned them away from the group, crowding 201 against the wall. To a passing Epsilon Internee, it would appear to be a confrontation of some kind.

"They will not be swayed, 201," whispered 277. "We cannot risk revealing the plan for fear that it will make its way back to the Officers. You knew the resistance to your idea would be strong."

201 shook her head. "It is no longer just my idea. You have seen the camp. 263 has seen it. We can live the way we all desire to live, without regulation. Why do they not listen to what they must know is the truth? There are questions that make no sense, until the answers are revealed. Surely they have questions, concerns. Do they never think of these matters?"

263 nudged 201. The conversation fell silent as a figure approached the line of Internees to the ration room, a blur of red followed by the somber black of an Officer's uniform.

277 breathed out in a slow hiss. "We are taught not to question, 201, that is regulation. You know what we face here. We were all birthed here. We were all taught to venerate the Pinnacle Officer and the Officers that protect us. It will take more than this to get them to understand. I had to pose the question as a theory, a hypothetical. If they believed that we were really planning to defect and turn against FERTS, they would take it upon themselves to expire us."

201 slapped the wall with her palm. "There must be a way. I will find it. Speak no more of this to the other Epsilon Internees. You have risked too much already." 201 pushed away from the wall, heading for the training room. "Say nothing else on the subject. Leave it to me."

"Wait, your rations!" 263 called out.

"This cannot wait," she muttered, breaking into a run.

201 edged through the door of the Epsilon training room, finding it empty.

"Reno," she whispered, breath hissing through her teeth. "Reno!"

"Yes?" Reno's voice startled her from behind. She turned around to find Reno by the door, a bundle of weapons slung over one shoulder.

"Reno, it's not working. It's not working!"

"Keep your voice down, 201. What do you mean?"

"263, 277 they have both tried. Nobody will listen to them. I will not be so foolish as to try it myself. I know the regard in which I am held here, venerated Fighter or not. They fear the outside. They fear the mercenaries. They do not understand that they are merely Officers in disguise. Why do they not listen, Reno? Do they wish to be expired?"

"It has only been a day, too soon to make any decisions. Would you have listened? That is, before you knew what you know now? Give them time. They don't know everything, 201."

"Well they should know. I do not wish for this to go on longer than necessary. Speak with Titan. Do something! I'm out of ideas." 201 ran from the training room.

"201, where are you going?"

"Rations," she called back. "I need my strength for training!"

Reno watched her leave, shaking his head and laying out the weapons for the first training session of the day.

10

That night, 201 collapsed, exhausted from the day's training regime. Reno had intensified her drills, paying her more attention than the other Epsilon Internees. She would have to speak to him regarding this, as it aroused suspicion. Perhaps they would need to commence training before the others arrived, in order to broaden her fighting skills.

She sighed and closed her eyes, sinking into the soft coverings of her bed. The piped music washed over her, the metronomic pulse keeping time with the beat of her heart. She felt her awareness slipping away.

She was running. The siren blared in her ears, but it could not harm her this time. She looked down to find her Implant Marker damaged, a gaping hole in her chest where it once had been, tendrils of smoke rising from the edges.

She rushed through the halls, searching for more Internees. She drew her bastard sword. Her plait bobbed against her back and a plume of ashes swirled in a trail behind her as she ran.

I have to get them out.

The siren rang out, throbbing in her head. Her mind swarmed with thoughts of guard Officers, of the Pinnacle Officer, a broken radio, a gash on her arm.

A scar. A scar. No going back to Omega now.

She ran through the hallways, triggering each door to open as she ran.

"Out! Everybody out!"

Go faster. Not enough time. No time!

Lines of Internees rushed past her towards the outer doors, towards the perimeter, towards the suspension zone.

"Get out! There is no time! Get out!"

More Internees pushed past her, scrambling for a way to escape.

She stood before another door, hair blowing as it sucked open.

"Go! Come on! You have to move!"

The Internee looked up at her. She sat at the edge of her bed, dressed in her Omega blue jumpsuit. Her hair was dark, her skin olive, her cat-like eyes fixed on her own.

They are my eyes.

A spot of blood lay on the sheet beside her. Beth 259201 smoothed her hair over her shoulder, sleek and well conditioned. Her nails were manicured. Her eyes were hollow, blank, unseeing. She held a bloodied nail file in her hand, but the blood was her own, the cut from her wrist dripping on the stone floor. Omega Beth 259201 remained in place, a remnant of herself, frozen in time.

"No, 201. I will stay. There are things I need to do. I belong here now. This place is a part of me. You cannot save me now."

"Get out! I won't ask again." 201 grabbed her arm but Beth 259201 did not move.

The siren blared in her ear, the urgency to escape overwhelming her. The walls seemed to shrink, sucking the air as it compressed around her.

She opened the next door, finding herself standing before a figure dressed in the red jumpsuit of Epsilon. Beth 259201 smiled up at her.

"I will see 232 tomorrow." Her voice was cheerful, lively. She polished a bastard sword in her hand, her palm riddled with cuts. "I need to make sure the weapons are oiled. I may be chosen to be a Fighter, you know. I have drills to run, techniques to learn. I must be ready."

"Out! Please! You must listen. You have to get out."

"No, I must wait for 232. She will be coming to see me. I look forward to seeing her again." Beth 259201 stared at the door, ignoring a fresh cut as she swept the cloth over the edge of the blade.

They are coming.

201 pulled at her sleeve. Beth 259201 would not move. Her body was heavy, somehow much heavier than her own.

The siren rang out again. The pitch seemed higher, the frequency of the signal more urgent.

The siren sounds different somehow. It sounds wrong. Changed.

She pushed out towards the stream of Internees, jostling for room. The Internees were panicked, changing direction, filing past her, spinning her around.

They're running the wrong way.

She felt a presence behind her, the hairs on her arms bristling.

"201. We have been waiting for you." The voices spoke in unison, amplified by their precision.

She turned to face them.

A line of Epsilon Fighters stood before her. Eyes blank, teeth bared, they raised their weapons at 201. She noticed a familiar face among them.

"263? Do you not remember me?"

263 looked through her, eyes fixed on a distant point.

"263?"

"We are gathered here to give thanks..." 263 advanced, brandishing her trident.

201 backed away as the Epsilon Fighters closed in. She ducked through the door behind her, hissing out a breath as it sucked shut. She leaned back on the door, hands gripping her bastard sword.

The silence in the room hung heavily in her ears.

A figure lay in the bed before her. This figure was small, too small to be a Vassal or a Fighter. The sheet covered her tiny body, obscuring her face. 201 stepped closer to the bed, reaching for the sheet.

Don't, 201.

She ignored her own warning, gripping the edge of the sheet and pulling the covers from the figure.

Don't, 201. Turn around, get out of here. You don't need to see this.

201 tightened her grip, pulling the sheet with one hand, feeding it through the other. The sheet seemed endless, the room too dark to make out any details of the figure beneath her.

No. I cannot leave now. I have to know.

A sliver of moonlight broke through the long window at her side. The moon was full, shining brightly on the perimeter, the tree line and the endless stretch of the suspension zone.

The corner of the face was illuminated, its skin dry and caked with dust.

Oh... she is just a little one. Expired. How could they leave her like this?

201 stepped forward, feeling the urge to run through the door and back to the hallway to face the Epsilon Fighters. The Fighters who had become unnervingly quiet.

The siren had stopped. The echo of the sound still rang in her ears.

She caught a glimpse of the face, partially eaten away with time, the skin leathery, crumbling, decaying.

Why is that face so familiar? I know that face.

201 stepped closer. A glint peeked out, illuminating a spot between the bed and the ragged uniform. 201 reached out, grimacing as she gripped the delicate shoulder, the skin disintegrating in her grasp as she turned it over, the body barely holding together under the tiny uniform.

No.

The body bounced against the bed, bones clattering, coming to rest on its back. The face stared back at her, hair scattered in sectioned tufts over the pillow, eye sockets hollow, cheeks sunken, teeth bared. The numbers blinked up at her, bright and garish against the ruined figure beneath.

Beth 259201 12Y.

11

"Line check!"

201 stepped through the doorway to join her fellow Epsilon Internees. The door sucked shut behind her, leaving the memories of her former self behind, at least for the moment.

She scanned the line of Internees while the FERTS Requital droned on.

201 had learned to tune out the sounds, focusing instead on her own thoughts. She remembered what Titan had told her about the symbol, about its significance to the wise ones from so long ago.

Will it be enough? What can it possibly do for us here?

She pondered the symbol. Would it be enough to strengthen her resolve? Would it make any difference at all? She had no answers. It was just a symbol, after all. Still, the image called to her, just as thoughts of the wise ones gave her a feeling of connection to the outside, while strengthening her connection to her inner thoughts as well. It also served to strengthen her connection to Beth #1, the first Beth. Bound to 201, just as Pinnacle Officer Wilcox was bound to her, along with all the Internees he had expired during his time in FERTS. Sometimes she wondered, with such a host of voices within her mind, vying for her attention, whether she was indeed senseless after all. Sometimes, she wished for nothing but silence.

So far, the other Internees had paid her no attention. She was known as a troublemaker, perhaps even a defective. Associating with a defective could be enough to earn Internee a reprimand of some sort, but being reported as a defective would surely send the Internee in question to Zeta Circuit. She was known as a defender of FERTS, and that was clearly an advantage, but it was unlikely to be enough to sustain her in her time at Epsilon. The influence of High Training Officer Reno was perhaps the only thing from keeping 201 from being sent directly to the scrapheap.

She followed the line of Internees to the rations room. The room was bustling with activity, talk of the upcoming Fighter selection being the topic of the day. She spotted 277's light brown hair amongst the crowd. 277's bench was crammed with 263 on one side and another Epsilon Internee pressed against her on the other side. The Internee's face looked vaguely familiar, though 201 could not place the context.

201 collected her rations tray, sliding into the empty spot on the bench opposite 277. One of the Epsilon Internees looked up, regarding 201 with a sneer. Beth 259255's hair was blonde, her green eyes tracking 201's movements as she sat at the table.

"I know you. You're the senseless one. You're the one who said we were all going to be expired and thrown in a pit." She glanced around the room. "We're still here, as you can see for yourself. And you're back in Epsilon. Again. Wasn't Omega to your liking?"

201 met her eyes. "I suppose I am better at fighting than I am at being a Vassal." She took a bite of her regulation protein, wrinkling her nose at the bland, watery taste.

"You are not even a Fighter," said 255. "Merely a fight trainee, only useful for weapons duty I suppose."

201 took another bite of her regulation protein. "Must one be a Fighter in order to be able to fight?"

255 shook her head. "There you go again with your senseless talk. You are making even less sense than last time."

"Ah, now I remember you," said 201. "Beth 259255, bastard sword champion."

"That's right," said 255. "And you are what, a bastard sword novice?" She smiled, giving 201 a wink.

201 shrugged, catching 277's eye, who quickly trained her attention on her tray, twirling her fork. 277 nudged 263 and both focused their attention on the rations before them.

"So tell me, 201," said 255, leaning forward. "For I have heard some strange stories about you. How was it that you came to be wandering through the suspension zone, hmm? Only the best Epsilon Fighters were sent to defend FERTS against the rogues. And you were a delicate Omega Vassal, hardly suitable for fight duty, let alone a journey to do battle with rogues. Where do you fit in to all of this?"

201 chewed her regulation protein, pondering 255's words. "I think... I think you ask too many

questions, 255. Isn't it true that an Internee that asks too many questions is likely to be sent to Zeta Circuit? That's what I heard, anyway."

255 scowled at 201. "I am surprised you have not yet been sent to Zeta. Last time I saw you, you were half clothed, making no sense as usual. You were trying to fight 277 at this very table. Now you wish to sit with us?" said 255.

"Perhaps I enjoy your company," said 201, breaking into a grin.

"I shall enjoy expiring you at the Epsilon Games, should you ever be selected as Fighter, though I doubt that will happen. How far away are you from 25Y, 201? Why, you must be the closest to over limit that I have seen in a long time."

201 banged her fist on the table, startling the surrounding Internees. "Why does it matter that I am nearly over limit? What does that mean, anyway? Who are you or anyone else to decide what is over limit?" She leaned closer to 255, their noses almost touching. 255 leaned back but 201 followed her movements. "Do you know what happens to the over limits? Do you know what happens to the Fighters who are defeated in the ring? There is no veneration, that is clear enough, at least to me. Do you know what happens to Vassal birthers when there is no more use for them?" She lowered her voice, gritting her teeth. "Do you know what happens to Zeta Internees?"

255 looked around at her fellow Internees for support. The surrounding Internees had turned away,

feigning nonchalance, but 201 could feel their attention honed on the altercation.

"Why should I care what happens to Zeta Internees? It makes no difference to me, nor should it affect any of us," said 255, pushing her tray to the side. "Zeta are the very example of how not to behave, that is why they are where they are, and why we are fortunate enough to have risen to Epsilon as venerated Fighters. Well, some of us, anyway."

"We are not fortunate," said 201. "And you should care a great deal about what goes on in Zeta Circuit, for that is where we will all end up eventually. If you were to be sent to Zeta, you would not know until it was too late. The reasons, there are so many reasons, none of which you can predict. If you were sent to Zeta, then, maybe then, you would understand what it means!"

255 turned to 277. "Are you going to listen to this senseless talk?"

277 shrugged. "I'm afraid 201 has a point. 263 and I have seen things on the outside that cannot be explained. Maybe you should listen to what she has to say."

255 looked at 263. "What about you, 263. Do you agree with this... defective's ramblings?"

263 refused to look up from her regulation protein. "I do not wish to draw attention to us with talk such as this. But yes, I agree with 201. I have found she has been right about many things, even though I do not always understand what she says."

255 grabbed her tray, pushing away from the table. "I think you are all senseless. You speak against what we have been taught, everything the Pinnacle Officer has bestowed upon us. I refuse to listen..."

"Wait," said 201, looking down at her tray. "You are correct, in a way." She heard 277's sharp inhale. "277 and 263... they were just humoring me. I know I am senseless, yet through the benevolence of the Officers at FERTS, especially High Training Room Officer Reno, I have been allowed the opportunity to rise to fight trainee, which for someone in my position, well it is truly fortunate. I will try to keep my senseless ideas to myself. I did not wish to offend the ideals of a fine facility such as this." 201 sighed, attempting a smile. She leaned her elbows on the table, resting her chin on her hands.

255's expression softened. She turned to 277 and 263. "You should be venerated for your efforts with the senseless one. I did not know that High Training Room Officer Reno had taken on such a difficult remedial task. You have my admiration, fellow Fighters." She left the ration room, nodding to 277 and 263 as she departed.

The rest of the Epsilon Internees filed out of the ration room, their uniforms blurring into a red mass. 277 caught up with 201 in the hallway, 263 following closely behind.

"What are you doing?" said 277, backing 201 against the wall. "Why did you say those things? 263 and I have tried so hard to make them understand! Now you dismiss everything that we have said? Why?"

201 peered over 277's shoulder, watching the remaining Epsilon Internees make their way to the training room. She lowered her voice, making sure the surrounding Internees could not hear.

"I said those things to protect you. 255 was ready to report us. It would be difficult, wouldn't you agree, to carry out the plan if we were all sent to Zeta Circuit. Especially if they decide..." She lowered her voice, leaning closer. "If they decide to move forward the scheduled incineration. It is clear the Internees will not listen. You were right. Everything they have been taught, everything we have all been taught, since we were little ones... it will take more, much more than this to make them understand. You must trust me on this. Say nothing more. It is not safe."

"We are running out of ideas, 201," said 263, glancing behind her as the last group of Epsilon Internees departed down the hallway. "We are also running out of time. It's not working, 201. It's not working!"

"Leave it to me," said 201. She pushed 263 and 277 aside, heading in the opposite direction to the rest of the group.

"The training room is that way!" shouted 263.

"Tell Reno I am unable to train today," she replied, heading for her quarters.

"I hope she knows what she is doing," muttered 277, falling in step with 263, heading for the training room.

12

201 arrived in the training room to find Reno collecting the weapons in bundles. The scent of stale sweat lingered in the air.

"I missed you at training today, 201," he said.

"I had to do some things. Important things," said 201. She collected a pile of weapons, following Reno to the weapons store room.

"You don't miss training. Especially not now. That is not negotiable."

"This was important, I thought I mentioned that."

"I don't care, 201. You train every day or not at all. Do you understand?"

"Yes, High Training Officer Reno," she muttered, sarcasm seeping through her words.

Reno turned to face her. "There will be none of that, either."

201 put down her bundle on the ready table in the weapons store room. "Reno," she whispered. "You must listen. I have found a way. Something to make them understand." She handed him a folded piece of paper, crudely drawn. "It is accurate. I know I remember this correctly. You must use this. It's our last chance."

Reno tucked the paper in his pocket, nodding. "This evening you run all the drills from yesterday. I will watch you to make sure you aren't getting sloppy on your technique."

201 stopped Reno on his way back to the training room. "Wait, aren't you even going to look at it? Not even once?"

"After your training, you will be on weapons duty," he continued, grabbing another pile of weapons and hauling them back to the store room. 201 blew out a breath, collecting another bundle and hurrying to catch up with Reno's strides.

"Wait, all of the weapons?" she called after him.

"All of the weapons. I trust you will not be skipping training again."

201 bit back her words, readjusting the bundle of weapons in her grip so as not to drop them. She took a deep breath, laying out the weapons on the ready table next to a stack of oiled rags. "No. No Reno, I will not be skipping training again."

"Good," said Reno. "Well come on then, you've got some drills to run."

13

201 returned from the rations room, perching herself on the edge of her bed. The regulation protein was unsatisfying, yet she felt her strength returning after the first training session with Reno, despite the added exertion of the following session with the rest of the Epsilon Fighters. Though she had complained at first, she had grown to enjoy training in secret, but still felt no closer to understanding Reno's methods. He spoke in ways that made sense, yet did not. Still, that was not a new development. She was not unfamiliar with senseless images, half-truths and obscured meanings. This was merely another facet of her development. Where it would lead was beyond her understanding.

She lay back on the coverings, rubbing at her collarbone.

I want this thing gone.

She closed her eyes, sleep overtaking her within moments.

201 tossed in her sheets, eyes darting right and left beneath her lids.

Beth stood before her, glowing from within. Her lips moved but 201 could not understand the words.

Her eyes conveyed meaning, though her mouth could not. Beth was weary. Beth needed to rest yet she could not.

She spread her arms, eagles circling her head. Her wrists opened, the blood spilling forth onto the ground, flowing into channels, snaking through the wood shavings of the Epsilon Fight Ring, through cracks in cold stone floors, feeding FERTS.

Her body withered, shriveling as the fluids drained out of her. She sank to the floor, dissolving as 201 watched, her own hand outstretched, unable to help.

The stone beneath her feet became saturated with liquid, a stinging, burning pool that burned the breath in 201's body, stinging her eyes and her nostrils. 201 squeezed her eyes shut, clenching her fists.

Find me, 201. Find me and let me sleep.

Without you, I cannot be free.

I am Beth, and I see everything...

I see.

I see.

I see.

See, 201.

See.

14

Reno and Titan crouched at the door of the rations supply unit.

"Do you know how to use this thing?" asked Reno.

"Yes," said Titan, hooking the equipment over his shoulder. "I have studied the manuals. I understand how it works. We must hurry, before the others wake."

Titan led the way out of the rations unit, keeping to the shadows. The sun had barely begun to rise, the majority of the ground blanketed in darkness.

"Here, Reno," said Titan, pointing at the beginnings of a path. "201's map leads us this way. Quickly, before the light comes."

Titan and Reno followed the path on the map as they ventured into the thickest part of the forest. Titan trudged through the trees, brushing shoulders with Reno as they stepped over rocks and fallen logs. The foliage was overgrown and hostile, slowing their progress. Titan broke away, walking a few paces ahead of Reno, muttering to himself.

"Yes, I see it! This is it. The rock that is shaped like the wheel of a cart. We are getting close." Titan stepped around the rock, kicking the branches away with the heel of his boot and heading off down a path that was not yet apparent to Reno.

"You sure you know what you're doing?" Reno caught up, falling into step with Titan, his voice pitched low.

"No. I do not. But I trust 201. She seemed to believe in what she was saying," said Titan, pushing away a branch that retracted, flicking Reno in the face. He stopped, rubbing his cheek.

Reno lowered his voice, glancing back at the thick forest behind them. "She seemed to believe? That's all you've got to justify this expedition? This is just great, Titan. I know you care for her, but you know they will expire us if they find us out here. We have no reason to be here."

"Calm yourself, Reno. There is no reason to speak softly. As you can see, we are far from any Officers out here. Except for ourselves, I mean." Titan grinned at him, raising his eyebrows.

"I'm glad you find this venture so amusing, *Officer* Titan. I wish to remain alive, that is all. I presume you would want the same for yourself."

"I know, Reno, but we do not have a choice. 201, 277 and 263 have tried everything else. This is the only way." Titan pulled away from Reno, looking for landmarks amongst the jumble of overgrowth.

Reno walked faster, attempting to catch up with Titan's strides, glancing around to ensure they had not been followed.

"You're going to get us expired," he muttered to himself, watching Titan step over logs and stray branches. "You couldn't have taken us down a path? Surely there is a path."

Reno arrived to find Titan holding a sapling out of the way, ushering him through to a clearing. He stepped through the gap, glancing up at the thick canopy above. "I don't like this, Titan."

"Yeah, me neither. I suppose we should be ready to fight if anything happens," he said, heading through the clearing.

Reno leaned closer to Titan as they walked side by side. "I am always ready to fight, Titan. You, on the other hand, could do with some training. Perhaps we will run evening drills, when the main training sessions are completed."

Titan slowed his pace, stepping over a gnarled tree root. "Don't you ever stop training?"

"No," said Reno. "Look out for any sign of movement. And be ready for anything, and I do mean anything. I don't know what we're going to find down here."

Titan moved to continue but Reno stopped him, raising a hand. Reno flinched, sniffing the air. He locked eyes with Titan as a foreign smell permeated the forest. A sickly, charred smell, pungent and sticky. The kind of smell that is impossible to forget. The kind of smell that filters through hair and clothing and will not leave. Reno knew that smell, from long ago, something he had never forgotten, but he would be surprised if Titan knew what it meant.

The sound of Titan's gagging broke the silence. A chill tore through him.

"Titan, where has she taken us?" Reno breathed shallowly, his heart rate spiking. He saw a break in the foliage up ahead where slivers of sunlight pierced through the leaves.

Titan groaned, sputtering. He leaned against a tree, his face pale.

Reno rushed forward, dimly aware of the forest opening out to a clearing. He stumbled to his knees, covering his mouth with his hand.

The ragged edges of the pit spread out before them, clumsily dug in a large, yawning circle. Bones lay piled against bone, scattered like twigs, the charred remains of flesh and clothing matted with dried blood. Emaciated limbs huddled together, bent at unnatural angles. Wisps of hair fluttered in the breeze, the acrid smell of burnt hair wafting from the depths of the pit. The layers of bodies stretched out, seemingly endless, the unnatural shades garish and bright in stark contrast to the muted browns and greens of the surrounding forest.

Reno caught a glimpse of an Internee jumpsuit peeking from the tangle of bodies, the familiar red of Epsilon still visible, riddled with tiny holes. Numerous heads lay severed, arms and legs bore wounds from swords and tridents. A face stared out from the dirt, her remaining hair a bright red, teeth bared, eyelids partially eaten away. A black and purple pattern ringed her neck, the shape resembling the imprint of fingertips. Her insignia glowed in the weak morning light, the numbers still visible.

Titan coughed, kneeling at the edge of the pit, eyes heavy with tears. "201 was right," he said.

Reno cleared his throat, blinking as a stray tear escaped.

"This is what they are to them," whispered Reno.

Titan nodded to himself, a hand covering his mouth as he took shallow breaths. Scattered amongst the remains of Zeta Internees were scraps of Kappa orange and Epsilon red, fluttering in the breeze. Peeking out from underneath these scraps were strips of white and blue. The jumpsuits of Beta and Omega.

Reno rose from his knees, turning back to Titan, who held the equipment away from his body, careful not to contaminate it with his vomit.

"This is Alpha Field," said Reno. His eyes scanned the breadth of the pit, shaking his head. "This is Zeta Circuit." He dropped his gaze to the ground. "This is on all of us now. You and me included." He blinked back tears, clearing his throat. "This is FERTS."

Titan hooked the equipment to a branch, heaving again.

"201 was right." Reno cleared his throat, wiping at his eye. "I should not have doubted her. 201 spoke the truth. She was never senseless. She knew what would come. She tried to warn us. She tried to warn them." His voice choked as he gestured to the pit.

Titan wiped his mouth, placing a hand on Reno's shoulder. "We didn't know. It doesn't matter now."

Reno shook free. "No! You are wrong. It matters more now. I should have known. I chose to ignore what I suspected but I could not allow myself to believe. I chose to believe what Pinnacle Officer Wilcox told me about the nature of things. I *chose* to believe in FERTS and look where it takes us."

He stared, tears forgotten, frozen in place. When he spoke, his voice was low, barely above a whisper. "She is in here, Titan. Beth 259179. 201 never told me because she wanted me to see this for myself. And my little one. I know it now." He stared at the pit, surveying its grisly contents. "They were sent to Alpha Field."

He turned, gripping Titan's arm. "You had better know how to use this thing." He unhooked the equipment from the branch, pulling it up to Titan's eye level. "Get it working."

15

201 gripped the sheets, head flinging to the side. She was drenched in sweat, the moisture seeping through the coverings.

The Epsilon wheel spun in her mind, the shades melding together as it turned faster and faster. The panels flew by too quickly to reveal the words. Games Operator Farrenlowe's flushed face peeked out from the middle of the wheel. Laughing, always laughing. 201 didn't need to see the words to know what they meant. There was only one word, repeated on every panel of the wheel.

Expired.

A chill prickled the back of her neck, spreading throughout her body.

"Spin the wheel and let chance decide!"

Games Operator Farrenlowe's voice echoed through her mind. The metallic tang of old blood assaulted her senses, mingled with the suffocating aroma of the well oiled cleaning cloth. The rub of grease on her palm felt familiar, yet... wrong.

"Spin the wheel and let chance decide!"

She rubbed the cloth over a sword, the markings familiar and comforting, her chosen weapon at Epsilon, her very own bastard sword.

The hilt was stained with blood, the new blood joining the old striations, highlighted in a deep brown, ingrained within the wood. The new blood seeped through the wood grain, tracing the whorls and streaks in a bright, garish red. The whorls looked familiar somehow...

"Spin the wheel and let chance decide!"

The wheel spun, gathering speed as it went.

Tick.

Expired

Click.

Expired

Tick.

Expired

Click.

The sound of the Epsilon Chance Wheel drowned out her thoughts, each click a physical jolt of electricity through her system, making the hairs on her forearm stand upright, wavering like a field of crops in a gentle breeze. Her Implant Marker burned within her chest.

Games Operator Farrenlowe stood in his usual spot under the lights, spreading his arms and pacing before the assembled crowd.

"Tonight we have an extra special treat for our honored Officers, for your tireless service to FERTS. Pinnacle Officer Cerberus is pleased with your dedication. To show his appreciation he has arranged a special fight for you. Our first Fighter, you know her, I know her..." He turned his head to 201. "Morton, Ryan and Jorg know her." He paused for the smattering of guffaws that followed. 201 bristled, gripping the cloth in her hand. She wiped the blood from the blade, the scent familiar to her.

It's my blood.

The cloth felt too bulky in her hand. She looked down to find her old sheet, a souvenir from her time at Omega, the single dark stain staring back at her, mocking her.

No.

She dropped the sheet to the ground, clasping her bastard sword, knuckles turning white.

"But her weapon of choice, now, how do we decide? The bastard sword seems a little unwieldy for such a delicate grip, wouldn't you say?" Another round of laughter emerged from the assembled Officers.

"A Fighter such as this deserves a weapon more fitting to the occasion..."

201 looked down at her hands. Her bastard sword was gone.

The nail file glinted in her outstretched palms, soaked in Pinnacle Officer Wilcox's blood. The laughter erupted around her. She looked at her hands once more, willing her bastard sword to reappear. Her hands began to shake, droplets of red falling on the wood shavings beneath her boots.

"So without further ado, let's welcome our newest, and most... unusual contender. She's a Vassal beauty, can't decide on whether she wants to fight or serve her Vendee, so what is there to say we can't let her do both? Win or lose, each of you Officers are free to take her and do with her as you wish." A violent cheer assaulted her ears.

She stared at the nail file in her hands, sharpened to a point by her own efforts, night after night in her chambers, with nothing but time to keep her company.

"So here she is, she's bad, she's deadly with a nail file, our very own Beth 259201! The cheer jolted her, all other sounds tuning out until all she could hear was her own labored breathing.

She looked up to find a row of seasoned Epsilon Fighters armed with spathas, tridents and bastard swords, her own bastard sword among them. She met the eyes of each of her opponents.

Something is wrong with them.

Their eyes. It was their eyes, no longer blue, green and brown, the middle of their eyes had widened until all that was left was black. Their pupils seemed to swim and swirl, drawing 201 closer to the endless blankness within.

They are no longer there.

One of her opponents smiled, her darkened eyes widening. She seemed to stare through 201, through her surroundings, fixed on an unknown point that 201 could not see.

Their mouths opened and closed in unison, too synchronized to be real.

"We are gathered her to give thanks... to Pinnacle Officer Cerberus and FERTS, for our provision and... bringing that little defective 201 back where she belongs! When we're finished with you, traitor, there will be nothing left to send to Zeta!"

201 stared, mouth going slack. Her nail file dropped to the ground at her feet. She fell to her knees, scrabbling through the wood shavings, droplets of blood tinting the curls of wood as she stretched her arms out, grasping, feeling nothing but wood dust.

"We give thanks to the Pinnacle Officer, the original, the highest, our beloved leader..."

201 scratched at her hands, attempting to dislodge the shavings adhering to her bloodied fingers. The voices became shrill, metallic, rising in volume.

"For showing us what happens to a Vassal who thinks she can be something else. Reprimand is not enough..." Their mouths opened and closed, but the voices were no longer those of her former Epsilon fellows, it was the voice of Pinnacle Officer Wilcox that reached 201's ears.

"She must... be taught a lesson!" They raised their weapons as one, a line of blades glinting under the garish lights of the Epsilon Games Ring. 201 attempted to stand, her wrist buckling under the weight of her body.

"Teach the defective!" The voice raised to a scream. "Teach the defective! Teach the..."

"Do not worry, 201," A cheerful voice rose from the shavings at her feet. Below her, behind her, down there... too low to make any sense, unless...

201 froze, her face tightening at the sound of a voice she did not believe she would ever hear again.

That voice.

201 pictured freckles, a mischievous smile and twinkling blue eyes.

No. It cannot be you.

"I said don't worry, 201." The voice came again from behind her feet, closer now, the sound muffled by the shavings. 201 froze.

Don't look. Don't look. You know what is down there. You know what it is. Don't look or you will see.

"Do not be afraid..." The severed head of her companion spoke again, its breath puffing the shavings at her feet. "We will be sure to venerate you when you are gone..."

201 screamed, leaping from the bed and throwing the coverings to the floor. She paced from one end of her quarters to the other, swinging her arms at an enemy she could not see. Her hands began to shake. She clenched her fists against the tremors, trying to calm her heartbeat.

Exhausted, she collapsed against the side of the bed, sinking in on herself and wrapping her hands around her knees. She stayed in the same spot, staring into the darkness, unblinking.

"232..." she whispered. "232..."

16

201 arrived early to meet Reno in the training room, eyes bleary.

"201," said Reno, unhooking a bastard sword from the rack, securing it in his grip. "You look terrible. Did you sleep?"

201 ran her hand through her hair, ignoring the question. "Let's get started," she said.

Reno nodded. "We're going to do something different today, before the others arrive." He turned around, motioning for 201 to follow. "Come on."

201 followed Reno to the back of the room, passing the racks of spathas, tridents, zulfiqars, and scimitars, ignoring them. Reno stopped, turning to face her.

"What are you doing, 201? Grab a weapon."

201 glanced around. "What do you mean? I don't understand. My bastard sword..." She reached for her weapon of choice. Reno pulled the sword out of her reach.

"Today I will be using the bastard sword. You will take your pick from the *other* weapons." 201 stepped back, surveying the selection. She reached out, gripping the first weapon that caught her eye. A scimitar. She held the dark wooden handle, her finger tracing its cracks, following the blood embedded in the grain. The blade was larger than expected, the point narrowing and curving at the tip.

"It's a little heavy in my grip," she said.

"Too heavy for you, do you think? That's the very reason why you're going to use it."

201 turned to face Reno, standing in Fighter pose, one leg slightly bent, the other extended, arms relaxed. She softened her gaze to allow for any peripheral movement.

Reno jabbed at 201, wielding the bastard sword in one hand. 201 blocked the move, taking a moment of extra time to raise the scimitar in the air. By the time she had reached the top of her swing, Reno had pulled the bastard sword in tight against his body, swapped hands from right to left behind his back and pointed the tip up at 201's throat.

201 sighed, lowering her weapon. "That was not a good result."

"Don't be discouraged," he said, lowering the tip. "Each weapon has its own movement, its own dance. The trick is to pick the right dance."

"Or the right dance partner," said 201.

"Yes. That is a factor. But the only thing you can control is your side, no matter who your opponent might be."

"So the scimitar is..."

"Well, you're still trying to use it like a bastard sword, which is to be expected. It is your chosen weapon, after all."

"But it's not a bastard sword," she replied.

Reno took the scimitar from 201's hand, swirling it in a lazy arc. "You can see, 201, it's not much heavier than your bastard sword, it's just weighted differently. Use that weight to your advantage, it will help your swing. You know what these blades can do. They are designed to slice and hew, not to stab. They are especially effective in removing body parts, including the head..."

201 squeezed her eyes shut, willing the image of 232's face to leave her mind.

"You must hit hard enough to split the skin, then drag the blade using its natural momentum." He sliced the blade through the air, drawing it to the floor. "Until it reaches its conclusion."

201 crouched on the ground, squeezing the point above her nose. "201? What are you doing?" said Reno, tapping her shoulder with the bastard sword in his other hand. "Pay attention!"

"Just... give me a moment, forgive me, Reno."

She felt the tip of the bastard sword wedge under her chin.

"You don't have a moment, 201. I know what is happening here. You have to ignore it and fight through."

201 pushed herself to her feet, snatching the scimitar from Reno's hand. She stepped closer, pointing the blade at his chest. "You know what is happening here? You mean you deliberately made me think of 232 to prove a point? What is wrong with you?"

Reno stepped back, raising the bastard sword to block her attack. "You think you are the only one who must bear what FERTS has done?" His voice cracked, though his face betrayed no emotion. 201 halted her movements. It was only then that she noticed the blue smudges beneath his eyes and the grey cast to his olive skin.

"You saw it. You saw the pit." 201 lowered her weapon, stepping towards Reno, hand outstretched. Reno batted her hand away with the tip of his sword. 201 scowled, slicing the blade at his arm. Reno blocked her advance with the bastard sword, stepping back once more.

"Good, good. You wish to attack now. That is good." He walked around her, prodding her with the bastard sword. "That's perfect for the next stage." He knocked the scimitar from her grip, its handle clattering to the floor. "Now, this time, you will fight me without attacking."

201 stood unarmed, staring at her scimitar on the ground, wincing at the jabs at her ribs from the sheathed bastard sword as Reno taunted her.

"Without... how do you expect me to fight without attacking? Why must you speak in senseless ways?" She pushed him away, pacing the floor and muttering to herself while Reno looked on, the hint of a smile at the corner of his mouth.

She stopped, turning to face Reno. "You mean defense. You wish for me to attack using only defense."

Reno nodded. "Sometimes, 201, the best attack is defense. Sometimes it is your only option." He took her hand, placing it around the handle of a shield. He stood back, raising the bastard sword, ready to fight.

17

201 collapsed onto the bed after her nightly drills. She ignored her need to shower, having grown accustomed to bathing less regularly at the camp. She had taken to bathing less frequently at FERTS as a result, and she made a point to resist the compulsion to bathe in regulation order.

Akecheta. The word seemed so distant once more. Some nights she wondered if the camp had been a dream, whether Raf and Cal and the others were real at all. She entertained the awful possibility that she had been alone in FERTS the whole time, seeing what might have been, or worse, seeing what never was.

She dragged the coverings over herself, tucking her hands behind her head. The piped music, bland and inoffensive, invaded her thoughts. She knew there was something more to the music, something that spoke to her mind on another level. She wondered if the other Internees felt it, the steady pulse of something she could not hear, but could only sense. She refused to get up to stuff the speaker hole again. Something in the drone of lilting nothingness was helping her. It fed her abilities, made them grow. She doubted the music had been designed with this in mind, but for her, it could be an asset to developing her sensibilities.

She closed her eyes, feeling the emptiness of the room descend. Her mind was clear, free from distractions, yet something was wrong. Often when she traveled in her mind, there was a signal, a feeling that came before the moment she broke away from her body. Sometimes it was a feeling of dizziness, sometimes it was a sound or a throbbing deep within her head. Sometimes it was a feeling of pulling back, retreating within herself before bursting forth into the unknown.

But tonight, something was different. Something was wrong.

Do you like it?

Wilcox's voice floated through her mind, a tinge of satisfaction in his voice.

"What do you want? You are not welcome here, Wilcox," she whispered.

That is where you are wrong, 201. I am back in my element. You brought me back to exactly where I needed to be.

201 flicked her eyes open, blurs of shapes emerging in the dark. "You did this. What is it? What have you done to me?"

Well, if you are so clever, you figure it out. I think you will find you are not special here, not that you ever were. I have made sure of it.

"What did you do?" She raised her voice in the empty room. She knew before she finished speaking that Wilcox would speak no more tonight.

She curled on her side, stuffing the pillow under her cheek. Something was not right with her mind, she could feel it. And Wilcox, he was different somehow. His essence was brighter, larger...

Stronger.

Something within FERTS was making Wilcox stronger. Whatever it was, it was something that was important to Wilcox in some way, perhaps a reminder of his former power. A symbol. Maybe something that symbolized his many achievements at FERTS.

She closed her eyes, trying to see, to hear anything that might assist her.

201's mind remained blank.

201's mind was never blank.

Clear, yes. Calm, perhaps. But this, this was an unfamiliar feeling. It was a sense of the ordinary, the daily order of FERTS, the regulation protein, the bathing, the dressing, the training. It was the feeling of being...

Ordinary.

What was it that Wilcox had said?

I think you will find you are not special here.

She squeezed her eyes shut, gathering all her energies to catch a glimpse of something, anything that would give her an insight into what Wilcox had done.

All she could see was the blackness of the inside of her eyelids. But there was something else. Something so faint, almost imperceptible. She could make out the outline of eyes. Eyes that she could swear were blue, even though she could not be sure. She tried to focus but the eyes remained out of reach, almost too distant to make out.

But the eyes did nothing. She saw nothing else, nothing of significance. The eyes didn't move, there were no voices, no hint of their meaning other than serving as a mere distraction on her way to a fitful sleep.

The eyes did nothing. They didn't even blink.

18

The next morning, 201 stared down the line of Epsilon Internees, the rows of red blurring in her vision.

The Officer stood at the railing, calling out the FERTS Requital with enthusiasm. "Internees of Epsilon. We are gathered here to send our gratitude to Pinnacle Officer Cerberus and FERTS, for our daily provision and protection from those who would strike against our Vassals, our Fighters and our Internees."

"We send our gratitude to Pinnacle Officer Cerberus and FERTS," came the reply. 201 kept her mouth shut, staring at the Officer. He stood proud, surveying the Epsilon Internees, failing to notice the one who did not speak.

201 made her way to the training room, finding Reno at the weapons rack, securing the weapons selection for the first training session of the day.

"Why aren't you in the ration room? I thought we agreed you need to eat as well as train."

"I eat quickly," she replied. She followed him as he headed to the weapons store room. The scent of cleaning oil and stale rags assaulted them as Reno unlocked the door.

Reno laid out three bastard swords on the ready table. 201 recognized one of them as her own weapon of choice. She reached for the sword.

"Not yet, 201. You have to train with all weapons."

"But this is my chosen weapon..."

"No, you must be versatile. You must be flexible."

"Flexible... I am not training for the Epsilon Games. You promised..."

"Shh, 201. Please keep your voice down. You know I would not risk you in the ring. We need you. Titan, 277, 263, they all need you. I need... I need you to train for all eventualities. This is how I train, and this is how you must learn. Trust me on this."

201 swallowed her words, picking up a trident, taking care not to remove the sheath. She turned it over in her hand, securing her grip with both hands. "I need to speak with you, Reno."

"What is it? Can it wait?"

"No, it cannot wait. I find this hard to explain but... Pinnacle Officer Wilcox has done something to me. He has closed off my mind, interfered with my thoughts somehow. I cannot see, I hear nothing when I try, only silence."

Reno sighed. "Pinnacle Officer Wilcox is expired, 201. He can't do anything to you now."

"No, Reno, that is where you are wrong! He has the power to ruin everything! He is bound to me, you know this! What will it take to make you believe? And now he is different, he is stronger here. Something here, within these walls, something inside FERTS has strengthened his essence and now my mind is blank. I see nothing now!"

Reno gripped her arm. "Have you lost your senses? Keep your voice down! If someone heard..."

201 shook him off. "I am sorry. I know you don't understand. Not everything, anyway. But this changes things. Changes the plan."

"You will think of something," said Reno.

"No, Reno," said 201, shaking her head. "Remember, you told me when I first trained with you, that I should use this." She tapped her head. "I need this to fight, Reno! It is my only advantage. I am not strong, I am not powerful. My only advantage is that I see things that others can not. That is my skill. Now it's gone and I have nothing!"

Reno placed a hand on her arm. "No, 201. That is not what I meant. When I said you should use your mind, I did not know of your other gifts. But it matters not. I saw your mind as it is. And your mind is still your most powerful weapon, no matter who your opponent may be. Focus your attentions on what you have right now, because that is all there is at any given time. Sometimes things do not go the way you expect. That is when you must adapt or be expired."

"Again, you make less sense than I do," said 201. "But don't you see, this changes everything! We are in danger, and now I cannot see what is coming."

"Then we will adjust. We are flexible, and versatile, or at least I am. You will learn in time."

"We don't have time! This changes everything! You speak of being versatile but what does that mean? Why must you make no sense?"

"You wanted to learn everything I know. I am teaching you everything, without leaving anything out. Come." Reno gestured for her to follow. "We have your training to commence. The rest can wait."

"I presume you are referring to more drills."

"Yes, 201. More drills."

19

The training room was filled with activity, Epsilon Internees gathering in groups, chattering and murmuring. Today was an important day, the day of Fighter selection.

201 stood at the back of the room, away from the other Epsilon Internees. She caught 263's eye, looking away so as not to draw attention to herself.

Games Operator Farrenlowe stood before them, cloak swirling at his feet. His voice carried the length of the training room as he gestured to the assembled fight trainees, arms outstretched.

"Epsilon fight trainees. Before we begin, we will send our gratitude to Pinnacle Officer Cerberus and FERTS, for our daily provision and protection from those who would seek to strike out against our Vassals, our Fighters and our Internees."

"We send our gratitude to Pinnacle Officer Cerberus and FERTS," the trainees replied. 201 was silent, noting that 263 and 277 also kept their mouths shut. She glanced over at Officer Reno, who refused to meet her eyes.

"Today may be the luckiest day of all," Games Operator Farrenlowe went on, his robes fanning out as he held out his arms. The Epsilon Wheel of Chance was positioned between Farrenlowe and a Beta Internee, dressed in her white jumpsuit, presentation smile in place. "Today is the day we find out who..."

"Will be the next Epsilon Fighters!" shouted the Internees. A ripple of excitement ran through the crowd, bursts of enthusiastic chatter rising up.

201 turned to find 263 and 277 flanking her on both sides. "What are you doing here?" she asked. "Are you sure you wish to be seen with me?"

263 stared straight ahead, watching Farrenlowe and the Beta Internee gesturing to the wheel, their smiles fixed firmly in place.

"Officer Reno looks troubled," said 263. "We came to find out what you know."

201 glanced at 263 from the corner of her eye. "I am not aware of anything that you do not know." She studied Reno's face, but he appeared no more or less stoic than usual. "Reno always looks like that." 201 chuckled, edging closer to the stage with 263 and 277 following closely behind her. Up close, 201 saw what 263 had spoken about. Reno's eyes looked tight, a pinched line between his brows forming. His jaw was clenched, a small twitch visible at the corner of his mouth.

"I don't like this," whispered 277.

"Me neither," said 263. 201 stared at the stage, the hairs on her arm beginning to rise.

"Are you ready to make High Training Officer Reno proud?" The crowd erupted in a cheer. Reno blinked, squeezing his eyes shut for a moment longer than usual.

"Are you ready to make Pinnacle Officer Cerberus proud?" The cheer grew louder, jarring 201's senses. A chill ran through her.

"Are you ready to join the venerated champions of the Epsilon Fight Ring?" The noise was deafening. Bile rose in 201's throat as Reno refused to acknowledge her presence. This was to be expected, 201 thought. There was no use drawing attention to their... collaboration? Alliance? What was Reno to her in all of this? But something about Reno's posture gave her pause. He stood in a way that projected a sense of unease, of... guilt?

Games Operator Farrenlowe grinned broadly as he gestured to the Beta Internee. The Beta Internee tilted her head, her presentation smile directed at the fight trainees. She held out the small metal bucket, turning her head from its contents. Farrenlowe put his hand in the bucket, pulling out a small piece of paper.

"201!" he called. The room was silent. 277's breath hitched. 201 could do nothing but stare at the Epsilon Chance Wheel, studying the varying shades of Epsilon red, blue, grey and green. Her hands and arms began to tingle, a dull pressure building in her head.

"Spin the wheel and let chance decide!" Farrenlowe's voice echoed throughout the room, the Beta Internee started the wheel with a flourish. The hollow tick and click of the wheel resonated in the silence.

201's blood rushed in her ears, a dizziness swaying her off balance. She planted her feet on the floor, sucking in air. Her stomach clenched, mouth beginning to water.

Tick.

Fight

Click.

Zeta Circuit

Tick.

Fight

Click.

Alpha Field

Tick.

Fight

Click.

Zeta Circuit

Tick.

The shades merged into a mass of brown as the wheel continued to spin.

Click.

Alpha Field

Tick.

Zeta Circuit

Click.

Fight

201 felt herself hoisted from the ground, the Epsilon Internees carrying her above the crowd. The dizziness overtook her as she swayed above their shoulders.

The room began to spin, unwanted memories surfacing of faces merging into a mass of skeletal remains, dried flesh clinging to bone, gaunt faces eaten away by insects. Games Operator Farrenlowe filled her mind, his shiny face laughing, spinning inside the wheel. 201 swallowed, the pressure in her head building until the rushing sounds overwhelmed her. She squeezed her eyes shut, pushing thoughts of that day in the ration room from her mind.

It was for today. What I saw then, it was for this day. It wasn't a warning for them... it was meant for me. Now I no longer see and it is too late.

Games Operator Farrenlowe smiled at 201. "Ah, but what is a Fighter without..."

"A weapon!" called the crowd. 201 teetered on 263's shoulders, supported by her fellow Epsilon fight trainees. She was a Fighter now, a duty of pride and veneration at Epsilon. The Epsilon fight trainees smiled up at her, all traces of their former animosity gone for now. She bobbed above the crowd as they carried her closer to the wheel that would choose her weapon. She caught Reno's eye, trying to convey her thoughts. He stared back, unmoved.

The Beta Internee gripped the second wheel, decorated in red and green. She flicked the wheel, releasing it.

Click.

spatha

Tick.

trident

Click.

bastard sword

201's shoulders sagged as she watched her weapon of choice pass by, the wheel slowing to a halt.

Tick.

shotel

Click.

scimitar

Tick.

spatha

The assembled fight trainees cheered, their voices disappearing against the hum within 201's head as she was carried above the crowd in a mass of red jumpsuits, the sounds of the crowd rising and falling in volume.

Not your chosen weapon, I see? Ah, 201. You are truly, truly unlucky.

201 ignored the voice of Pinnacle Officer Wilcox inside her head. She fixed her eyes on Reno, narrowing them.

How could you...

Reno closed his eyes, giving an almost imperceptible shake of his head as the crowd carried 201 from the training room in veneration.

20

Later that evening, 201 sat in the ration room, perched on the bench between her fellow Epsilon Fighters. She felt a nudge at her ribs.

"Are you not excited, 201? You are a Fighter now! And so close to over limit as well. You have finally achieved a position worthy of veneration!"

201 ignored the comment, scowling at her ration tray.

"What about you, 277? Are you looking forward to the chance to face 201 in the ring? Or should I say, defeat 201 in the ring?" The Epsilon Fighters erupted in laughter around her.

201's eyes widened. She glanced across at 277, her chosen opponent, it seemed. 277 refused to look up, concentrating instead on her extra rations of regulation protein, one of the perks from her recent selection as Fighter. 201 finished her rations quickly, conscious of her need for strength. Since returning to FERTS and subsequently to Epsilon, her muscle mass had increased significantly, yet she lagged behind her fellow Fighters in stature and strength. She watched 277's formidable bicep begin to tense as she gripped her fork.

"I relish the opportunity to make Reno and the Pinnacle Officer proud. I am thankful for the chance to prove my worth as a Fighter at the Epsilon Games." 277's voice was dull, uninflected. She stared at her empty plate, fork clattering as she left the rations table. 201 pushed away her plate, following 277. She caught 277 at the door, gripping her elbow.

"277, I do not wish to fight you. You are my companion. There must be another way."

277's eyes were blank when she met 201's gaze. "There is no way out of this, 201. I must expire you. I have no choice. It is either you or me, and I do not plan on being expired at the Epsilon Games."

201 watched as 277 strode out through the doorway, disappearing down the hall.

201 sat in her quarters at Epsilon, perched on the end of her bed. She leaned her elbows on her knees, brows drawn together. If she could no longer see what once had been accessible to her, she would have to use her other faculties, such as logic and deduction. She pondered the wheel, thoughts rushing through her head.

There was something about the wheel, something that seemed less random that it should have been. All chosen fight trainees had been rewarded with their weapon of choice from the spin of the wheel, save for 201 herself. Using logic alone, this was unlikely. It made sense that each and every chosen Fighter would be matched with their own weapon to facilitate the most entertaining bout for the Officers. It all came back to the Officers, as the Epsilon Games were held for the benefit of the Officers and the Officers alone. So the Fighters had received their chosen weapon, why did that matter?

Think, 201.

277 had been awarded her own weapon of choice, her zulfiqar. 201's prowess with the spatha, or lack thereof, was no match for 277's seasoned zulfiqar skills. Why indeed, did it matter that 201 had not been awarded with her very own bastard sword, her weapon of choice? It was unusual, that much was clear, but what reason could there be for the unfamiliar weapon to be awarded to her, if not to...

Sabotage

What other reason could there be aside from hindering her efforts in the ring? Perhaps there was another reason, one she could not comprehend. But the more 201 thought on the matter, the more she understood. She had been awarded a weapon foreign to her because she had been chosen to fail. She had been matched with a far more experienced Epsilon Fighter, who had subsequently been awarded with her own weapon of choice. The Officers desired blood, and through this mismatched fight, they would no doubt receive it. Unless she could think of another reason for this development, it would seem that Reno had betrayed her.

201 edged back to rest her head on the pillow. No images came to her mind, no voices lulled her to sleep. Her mind remained blank. She stared at the sliver of moonlight through her window and felt nothing.

21

Reno made his way through the darkened hallways of Epsilon. He stood at the doorway to Games Operator Farrenlowe's quarters, putting his ear against the door. The sounds emanating from within deterred him from knocking. The Games Operator was entertaining a Vassal, or rather, it may have been the other way around. He had initially planned to speak with Farrenlowe regarding the unusual Fighter selection for the Epsilon Games as he had felt an uneasiness since the first moment he had awoken. Something seemed wrong and he had experienced a sense of dread for the first time in all his time as High Training Room Officer. Now, he believed he had good reason to feel unease.

He paced outside the door, chiding himself for considering for a moment that Farrenlowe would be forthcoming with the details. He could not reveal his intentions, especially not to one as powerful as the Games Operator. The Vassal, it seemed, had saved him from risking the plan with foolish questions.

He pushed away from the door, heading to the Epsilon Games Ring. He had no reason to be there save for his purpose of investigation. Should the topic come up, he would have to think of something. He unlocked the door, slipping inside. He knew that he had purposefully omitted 201, 277 and 263 from the Fighter selection list. Whatever had been done was beyond his control and he did not appreciate the Games Operator bypassing his authority to achieve the desired result.

He passed bags of sawdust shavings, ignoring the stench of stale blood and cider. The walls, the floors, they would always smell this way, he supposed. He spotted a door to one of the many store rooms and paused at the entrance. Why was it that he had never thought to investigate the wheel? He supposed it was not his concern, certainly not relevant in his list of duties. Yet something was clearly wrong. He had to know.

He found the wheel at the back of the store room. It looked ordinary, and nothing appeared to be amiss. He had no reason to investigate further, but he couldn't forget the look on 201's face when she was selected as Fighter. He remembered her eyes when she understood her fate.

He stepped closer and gave the wheel a spin. The click of the wheel broke the silence in the room.

Tick.

Fight

Click.

Zeta Circuit

Tick.

Alpha Field

The wheel continued its journey, ticking and clicking before coming to rest in its final location.

Tick.
Zeta Circuit
Click.
Fight

Reno ran his hand over his face. Perhaps it was a coincidence. He gave it another spin, then another. After three times, the final result was the same as the first. He could not produce a different result, no matter how many times he tried.

Fight

Fight

Fight

He uncovered the second wheel behind the first, giving it a spin, hoping that he was wrong about his suspicions. 277 was the last Fighter subject to the Epsilon Chance Wheel and her luck at being awarded her own weapon of choice was celebrated throughout Epsilon. The panels merged to a brown shade as the weapons flew by, landing on 277's weapon of choice.

zulfiqar

He gave the wheel another spin, then another. The result was always the same, landing at the same spot after every spin.

zulfiqar

zulfiqar

zulfiqar

He felt along the back of the wheel, finding an extra large notch. A means of movable, replicable selection. He huffed out a breath, covering the wheels and making his way out of the Epsilon Games Ring.

The fights are fixed, he thought. How could I be so foolish not to see, not to understand? It was not my concern, it was never my concern. The fights are fixed and now 201 is in danger of failing.

No, not just 201. The plan. The whole plan is in jeopardy.

22

The knock sounded on Reno's door later that evening. He opened the door expecting to find Games Operator Farrenlowe or one of the guard Officers, but instead, the hall appeared empty. A flash of red ducked under his arm. He turned to find the door swinging shut behind him and 201 standing in his quarters, her hands clenched at her sides. He sucked in a breath, backing against the door.

"201... I didn't betray you. You have to believe me."

201 stared at Reno, refusing to move. "They cannot select me for Fighter unless the High Training Officer, that is, you..." She poked at his chest. "Unless you had been the one to put me up for selection. Unless you were the one to put 277 up for selection. We have no choice but to fight now, and one of us will be expired. Why would you do this Reno? Why would you threaten the plan in this way? Were you offered a reward?"

"No, 201." He gripped her hand, pushing it away. "I did not put you up for selection. I suspect it may have been Games Operator Farrenlowe, or perhaps the orders came from higher up. The orders may have come from Pinnacle Officer Cerberus himself."

"I cannot expire 277, Reno. She is my companion."

Reno clenched his jaw. "You must, 201. If you spare her, or if she decides to spare you, the fighting creatures will be released and both of you will be lost. You know this. How could you consider this? We need you, 201."

"We need 277 as well!"

"One of you must fall. That is the regulation."

"You know what I think of regulations," said 201. She glanced around, taking in her surroundings. "These are your quarters? Hmm. They are pleasing and comfortable. Little wonder you were so reluctant to believe me."

"201, listen to me. The wheels are rigged. The result is fixed. I did not put you or 277 up for selection. There is another reason for this and I am afraid it is beyond our control."

201 sighed, seating herself on the corner of Reno's bed. "It matters not. That is not why I came here tonight Reno."

Reno raised an eyebrow. "Why are you here, 201?"

She placed a hand to her chest, tapping her collarbone. "I need something. A metal. I do not know what I search for but I will know it when I see it. I need it now. There is no time left. We have no chance if I do not get what I require tonight. Before my mind was closed off, I saw how the Implant Marker would be affected. This metal is the only way to shield the Implant Marker."

Reno crouched on the ground beside 201. "What type of metal?" he asked.

"Just tell me what you know, Reno. My time is running out."

Reno's shoulders slumped. He pulled out his keys, handing them to 201. "There is a place. The stores underneath Kappa Circuit." He looked up to find 201 pulling the door shut behind her.

23

201 unlocked the store room, surveying the junk inside. Many of the items were covered in a thin layer of dust, the room smelling of damp and neglect. She rummaged through boxes of wires, various electrical parts and other items that she did not recognize by sight. She knew what she needed to find in order to carry out her plan, but she had no guarantee of finding it in the mess she saw before her. She sighed, lifting another box and removing its contents, piece by piece.

An hour into her search, she caught a glint of something familiar. The strips were secured in rolls, a strange, flexible metal that crumpled when she pinched it between her fingers.

This is it. This is what I need.

A thin sliver of light peeked in through the doorway. 201 held the roll to the light, watching as it glinted pink, then orange. 201 removed her jumpsuit, allowing it to fall to her waist. She unwound the roll, winding it around her shoulder and upper chest, ensuring that it covered her collarbone. She continued to wind the roll underneath her arm and back around her collarbone once more. She refastened her jumpsuit, checking her range of movement. The metal was cold. It pinched a little, restricting full range of movement in her left arm. It was not ideal, but she could learn to work around it. It would have to do.

She grabbed two more rolls, concealing them underneath her clothing and slipped the door shut behind her. She checked the halls but they were deserted. The Officers clearly had other priorities than hovering around the store rooms underneath Kappa Circuit.

201 rubbed at her shoulder, wincing as she shuffled away from the stores beneath Kappa Circuit, adjusting the rolls beneath her jumpsuit. The halls were dark, most of the Officers asleep in their quarters, with the bulk of the guard Officers posted around Pinnacle Officer Cerberus' quarters. 201 edged her way down the hallway, heading towards the ration supplies unit. She slipped through the crack in the door, wedged open as it had been before. She stepped upon the earth, pushing herself forward.

I need to test it, she thought to herself, sprinting to the edge of the field, feeling the breeze whip against her face. She turned when she neared the tree line, running back to the ration supplies entrance. She looked up at the observation tower, noting that the alarm had not yet been raised.

The beacon should have sounded out by now. I'm undetectable. They can't track my movements.

She sprinted another few times to make sure her theory was correct, hearing no sounds of disturbance or alarm. There was nothing but the gentle breeze against her cheek.

Don't be so sure, she thought. Perhaps I was lucky this time. Try again. You have to try again.

She crouched, sucking in a breath. She took off towards the trees, pumping her arms by her sides. The metal pinched against her arm but she ignored it, touching a tree and turning back, heading for the ration supplies unit. She paused at the door, panting.

You should run, 201. Just like you did before. They can't track you, so why stay?

Pinnacle Officer Wilcox's suggestion jarred her. If he was to suggest such a course of action, then she should do the opposite, that much was clear to her. She thought she had detected a change in his voice. Perhaps she had imagined the note of fear in his words.

She gave it one last try, running towards a tree and touching the bark, gripping it with her fingers. She pushed off the tree, hiding in the grass and glancing up at the observation tower. The siren had not sounded as yet.

She thought of the possibility of running. It was tempting, she thought, as she crouched in the longer grasses near the tree line. She could leave now, leave FERTS behind and be free of everything she faced within those walls. She looked back at the facility, unassuming from the outside, hiding the true nature within.

She thought of Raf and Cal and the others, who would welcome her back to the camp without question. She remembered the warmth of the cabins, the scent of the open fire. She remembered the sounds of the waterfall at night, the beauty of the towering cliffs, days spent training in the fields under the sun and nights gathered around the fire, drinking indigestible cattail spirits. She chuckled to herself. She missed her companions. She missed the open spaces, the sound of laughter. No line check, no regulation order, no...

201 stood, hands grasping the bark of a tree, feeling the pebbled grain under her fingers. The moon was almost invisible, a sliver of light under a bright canopy of stars.

She took a step towards the suspension zone. Before she could take another step, she thought of Reno's face, of Titan and her companions in Epsilon. Reno would not begrudge her this, nor would Titan. She would not be forced to fight her companion 277. Perhaps there was another way. No. She could not think of that, not now.

201 sighed, pushing away from the tree line.

They needed her, that was the truth. What needed to be done must be done from the inside. Her companions could not do this without her. She could not risk the plan for her own safety. She strode back through the field, heading for the wedged door of the rations store, a sliver of artificial light peeking through the crack spilling out on to the grass below.

She would return to FERTS, and she would fight 277 in the Epsilon Games Ring.

There was no other way.

24

201 sat alone in the Fighter's dressing room, listening to the sounds of muffled applause and jeers seeping through the door. The rooms were small, designed for one Fighter only to prevent the unwanted development of one Fighter expiring another before the bout had even begun. 201 gripped the spatha in her hand, flexing her fingers. The special Fighter's meal lay untouched on the dressing table. The food was unfamiliar, yet looked delicious. She knew she should eat, she needed the energy, but her stomach had clenched at the sight of it. She pushed away the plate, swallowing the nausea that welled up within her.

She remembered her days in the weapons store room, polishing the blades with the stale rags dipped in oil. Now the scent reached her nostrils, not from a cloth, but from her own blade. The one she would use against 277 in the Epsilon Games Ring.

A cheer rose up, filtering through the doorway. The fighting creatures were entertaining the crowd, the high pitched yelps of the creatures as they dueled jolting her from her thoughts.

Soon. There's no getting out of this. Soon it will be my turn.

She stared at her reflection in the mirror, willing Beth to come to her, to provide words of reassurance. She thought of the wise ones, hoping for some kind of guidance. She tried to focus her mind but the thought of 277 and her zulfiqar clouded her thoughts. The words that came were not welcome to her ears.

You should not have come back, 201. Look at you now. You are not suited to this, you never were. You're a weapons duty Internee, nothing more. You will be expired within moments against a seasoned Fighter.

"You sound so sure," she muttered, feeling foolish for speaking to Pinnacle Officer Wilcox aloud.

I am sure. You will see how sure I am when the time comes. I shall enjoy watching 277 expire you. A fitting end, don't you think?

"Why can't you stay expired?" she whispered.

She stood, facing the mirror, adjusting her leather breastplate. She had covered her shoulder with cloth, wrapping the strips of metal beneath. Her leather skirt sat high on her thighs. She attempted to pull the layers of leather to cover more of her legs but it was pointless. Each time she moved, the leather pulled apart to reveal more than she expected. She supposed it was a small matter compared to what she faced in the ring. She stared at her reflection, eyes smudged in black cosmetics, hair braided at the sides and left untouched and wild at the back. Her feet pinched at the toes, the sandals too tight with their crossed leather bindings snaking around her calves. She flexed her toes, grimacing.

I should be wearing the clothing of a free warrior, not this, she thought to herself. She stared at her reflection in the mirror one last time, waiting for a sign, something, anything that would stop this from happening.

She stared into the mirror, narrowing her eyes at her reflection. She grabbed her shield, hoisting her spatha firmly in her grip and opened the door to the flood of cheers and whistles from the Epsilon Games Ring.

25

Games Operator Farrenlowe spread his arms, gesturing to the Officers seated before him. The assembled crowd of faces stared expectantly, eyes wide and slightly glazed. His cloak brushed the ground as he gestured, wood shavings adhering to the hem.

"Welcome, esteemed Officers to the monthly routine Epsilon Battle!" Cheers filled the hall arena, as cider mugs clinked together. The Epsilon pledge-takers moved silently throughout the crowd, collecting wagers from the Officers and carefully avoiding the frequent splashes of cider from the generously filled mugs.

Farrenlowe held a finger to the air, signaling for calm. The sleeve of his cloak peeled down his arm, revealing glimpses of the burgundy lining glinting under the heat of the Games Circuit lights.

"I ask you to stand for the FERTS Requital." The Officers stood, rising with their cider mugs held high. As the chatter quieted, an unusual calm descended on the gathering of Officers.

"Esteemed Officers, Fighters of Epsilon, menial Internees. We now send our gratitude to Pinnacle Officer Cerberus and FERTS, for our daily provision and protection from those who would seek to strike against our Vassals, our Fighters and our Internees."

"We send our gratitude to Pinnacle Officer Cerberus and FERTS." The crowd replied, the murmurs jumbling into chaos as the Officers resumed their drinking and chattering. 201 stood at the side of the ring, breathing slowly, counting to nine to calm herself. She handed over her shield and spatha to the Fighter attendants beside the ring. One of the attendants smiled, giving her a nod. She could not smile back.

"We have a special treat for you tonight... she's a first-timer, former Vassal..." he paused to allow for the shouts and hollers that rose from the crowd. "Celebrated defender of FERTS and brave defeater of rogues, she's a master of the bastard sword, but trying her hand at the spatha tonight, it's our very own Beth 259201!" The cheers echoed through the hall arena, shrill whistles and the clink of cider mugs filling the air.

201 took a deep breath and ducked her head through the sharpened wire, grabbing her shield and spatha from the two mail-gloved Fighter attendants and waving them away with the back of her hand. Her feet kicked up a mass of shavings in the ring, the plume rising and falling to the ground, sparkling under the lights. The metal strips were cool against her skin, biting against her as she moved.

She stood, scanning the faces of Officers in their dark uniforms, menial Internees and Epsilon pledge takers weaving among the rows, recording each wager with quiet attentiveness. She glowered at them all, her teeth flashing through her mass of brown hair, her hazel eyes gleaming, shining under the lights. She smiled at the crowd, raising her spatha. The crowd roared. A strange sense of calm washed over her as she adjusted her grip on her shield, securing it firmly in place. She held her body in Fighter pose, awaiting the arrival of her opponent. Games Operator Farrenlowe raised his arms, gesturing for quiet.

"For tonight's challenger, we welcome another of our beloved Fighters. She's a defeater of rogues, master of the zulfiqar, the reaper of the ring, she's the terror with the light brown hair. It's our very own Beth 259277!"

201 inhaled sharply, willing her body not to tense. She remained in Fighter pose, aware and alert.

277 bowed her head, two Epsilon Internees holding apart the sharpened wire with their mail gloves to allow her to enter the Epsilon Games Ring. Her leather armor lay heavily on her frame, the breastplate stitched tightly for protection rather than show. Her leather skirt scratched above her knees, the layers splitting apart as she moved. The shavings swirled around her leather boots, fluttering to nestle in the straps as she stilled to adjust her shield. 277 raised her zulfiqar high above her head, nodding to the crowd. A cheer erupted as 277 turned to each corner of the hall arena, the light catching the glint of the split-bladed sword as she smiled, narrowing her eyes at the mass of faces before her. The Officers

shouted and jeered, their cheeks flushed from the effects of the cider.

277 held her zulfiqar high in the air, turning it under the lights. The crowd cheered, clinking their cider mugs and placing their last-minute wagers. 201 noted the familiar stripe of dried blood ringing the hilt, marking it as 277's weapon of choice. According to the wheel, 277 was indeed lucky, 201 thought, and her fellow Epsilon Internees had confirmed this development with great enthusiasm. 277 smiled, meeting 201's stare. From the look in 277's eyes, it appeared she believed that luck had favored her in this battle.

I do not wish to fight you, 277. Please, there must be another way.

The heat in the hall arena thickened the air, intensifying the stifling smell of blood. The stale remnants of Epsilon Fighters from days past remained ingrained, the spatters and drips from the old battles lingering in the cracks of the stone floor, infusing the walls, the rows of tiered metal seats and the sharpened wire surrounding the ring. The sickly metallic tang permeated the air, filtering through the dark suits of the assembled Officers, nestling amongst the wooden crates that housed the fighting creatures and surrounding the metal-banded cider barrels lining the walls.

One of the fighting creatures snarled, its sharpened fangs snapping at a menial Internee who had unwittingly ventured too close to the cages. The Internee shuffled away, clutching the handfuls of wagers close to her red jumpsuit as she weaved back through the assembled Officers.

201 shrugged off the chill creeping down her back. The fighting creatures were a trifling diversion from the main fights, an aside to keep the Officers entertained while the new Fighters prepared for the next battle, but 201 knew from experience what a fighting creature could do when freed from the leash.

277 played to the crowd, tracing her gloved finger along the serrated blade of her zulfiqar, feigning shock as her fingers caught on the twin points at the tip. The crowd jeered and bellowed as 277 cast a final nod at 201 before standing in regulation Fighter pose. Her arms hung loosely by her sides, right leg outstretched, body alert, eyes trained straight ahead. 201 mirrored her pose, her eyes never leaving 277.

Games Operator Farrenlowe adjusted the FERTS games insignia around his neck. The familiar shield-mounted symbol of a sword crossing a spear snagged on his robe, tearing a small hole in the material as he freed it to hang prominently on his chest.

"It begins!" Farrenlowe cried, retreating from the ring with a flourish amongst shouts and applause from the crowd.

201 swallowed, her throat dry from the stifling heat. The two menial Internees sounded the gongs, signaling the fight to commence. 277 towered over her, moving with the ease of a celebrated Epsilon Fighter. She glanced at Reno out of the corner of her eye. He caught her eye for a moment, a look passing over his features that 201 could not decipher.

What was I thinking? I cannot fight her. She has her chosen weapon. I have nothing but a spatha to defend myself.

The rounded tip of her spatha appeared blunt compared to the streamlined points of 277's zulfiqar. Spathas were clumsy in her experience, unwieldy and heavier than her chosen bastard sword. 201 longed for her chosen weapon, its familiar handle and delicate blade at her fingertips.

201 steeled herself, turning her gaze to 277's eyes, her own eyes narrowing in challenge. She watched 277's chest rise and fall, holding her stance, waiting for the first sign of movement from 201. From the corner of her vision she spotted Games Operator Farrenlowe toying with a box, a device that held some kind of dial that he twisted in his hands.

What is that...

277 clutched at her chest, stumbling back before righting herself and standing once more to her full height. 201 glanced at Games Operator Farrenlowe, watching the smile spread across his broad features. 277 looked down at 201, her eyes morphing to pools of black, staring through 201. 201 gripped her own chest, glancing around at the crowd. She felt nothing but the pinch of the thin metal strips digging into her skin.

277 smiled. It was not the smile of an Epsilon Fighter in the throes of entertaining the crowd. This was the blank smile of nothingness. The 277 she had known was no longer standing before her.

277 whispered words that only 201 could hear. "I shall expire you, 201, in the name of FERTS." Her brow creased, jaw clenching. "You cannot stop me now." The words sounded sure, yet they were regretful, somehow.

201 lunged, faking to the right and swerving to charge 277 with her spatha angled to the left. 277 anticipated the move half-heartedly, flicking her zulfiqar at the spatha's blade, neutralizing the maneuver in a single movement. The crowd whistled and jeered. A cider mug flew through the air to fall at 201's feet. She kicked it away with the heel of her boot, scattering a cloud of shavings into the air, her eyes never leaving her opponent.

She's stronger. Too strong. What have they done to you, 277?

She saw two figures rising to their feet, eyes wide. Reno stood to attention, watching 201's moves and shaking his head. Titan moved in the corner of her peripheral vision, his body tense, hands clenched by his sides.

No distractions, 201 thought to herself. Do not look at them. Keep your eyes on your opponent.

277 laughed, twirling her zulfiqar lazily and playing to the crowd. The jeers and shouts filled 201's ears but she kept her eyes soft, trained for any sign of unexpected movement. Before 201 could move, the zulfiqar shot out, glancing 201's arm. 201 staggered back, almost losing her footing in the wood shavings gathered at her feet, watching the blood drip against her leg. She scampered to the edge of the wire,

keeping 277 in her vision at all times. 277 laughed, pacing the ring to the cries of the Officers in the crowd.

I cannot defeat her. She is toying with me, merely putting on a show for the Officers. Soon, she will finish this.

201 glanced down at her shield. The brown embossed leather sheath was fastened in place with studs that caught the light as they moved and the surface was interlaced with layers of a thinner, more delicate leather. This layer was black, intricately fashioned in a curved leaf pattern, the lines swirling to frame the outer rim of the shield. She swung the shield, feeling the weight on her arm, a distant thought forming within her awareness.

277's eyes tracked the movement of the shield as it swayed in 201's hand, momentarily transfixed.

The words of Reno came to 201's mind.

Sometimes, the best attack is defense. Sometimes it is your only option.

201 trained her mind to close out the noise from the crowd, the smiling face of 277, the smirk on Games Operator Farrenlowe's face. Her mind retreated to a place of calm, a place of one thought and one thought only.

She lunged forward, swinging her spatha, deftly flicking out at 277's neck as 277 snaked away, twisting her body to face 201 once more.

201 charged, hearing 277's sharp intake of breath. She began to swing the spatha in an arc, blade flashing towards 277 in a blur of silver. 277 narrowed

her eyes, focusing on the silver of 201's blade, just as 201 hoped she would.

As 201 swirled the blade towards her, 277 saw the opportunity to thrust upwards at 201's unguarded chest, crying out in triumph as her double-pointed blade struck. The crowd screeched in triumph, the fighting creatures barking in agitation from their wooden crates.

A chill ghosted over 201 as time slowed and narrowed.

The cheers from the crowd faded from her ears as she stared the glint of 277's zulfiqar under the lights.

A single curled shaving floated past the hilt of the blade, each groove and striation of the roughly planed wood standing out in brilliant relief as the shaving twirled and danced in the air.

277 shifted, gripping the handle of her zulfiqar, desperately trying to dislodge her weapon. Her zulfiqar was rigid, both points of the tip firmly buried in the thick leather of 201's shield. As 201 had hoped, 277 had been training her attention solely on the swirling movement on the spatha, but not the answering movement of the shield from 201's other hand.

277 tugged once more, shimmying the hilt in an attempt to free the serrated blade. Her eyes traveled along the curved shaft of her zulfiqar, scanning up to meet 201's eyes.

Do not do this, 201. This is not necessary. You have proved your worth.

201 ignored Pinnacle Officer Wilcox's words, for the very reason that he was right. But as 201 looked into the eyes of her former companion, she saw the relentless spirit of one who would expire until there were no more left to expire, all in the name of FERTS. She watched the smile of Games Operator Farrenlowe, the pinched look on Reno's face and the paleness of Titan's skin as they tracked 201's movements.

It's either you or me, 277, they will not let this fight end without victory. I cannot let you expire me. I could have run, but I must do what I came here to do. If I spare you, you will expire me and everything we have fought for is lost.

Another voice broke through her mind, almost too quiet to hear. It took her a moment to understand the origin of the voice.

277 looked up at her, a flash of her companion's true nature breaking though the haze of blackness in her eyes. She gritted her teeth and repeated the words. "Do it," she whispered. "Do it!"

201 plunged the spatha through the side of 277's armor. 277 sank backwards, her head tilting to the ground. She ventured one last futile kick to the shield, tugging on the handle of her weapon.

201 bent down to 277, whispering words of apology, tears stinging at the corners of her eyes.

Games Operator Farrenlowe stood, packing away his box and setting it to the side.

277 sighed, her pupils contracting to their former size as she looked up at 201. She chuckled, a spot of

blood landing on her chin. "You were right," she murmured.

201 bent closer to hear 277's words. "I still remember it, that day in the ration room so long ago..." 277 raised a hand to shield her eyes from the lights. "I thought you were senseless but you knew."

"I don't understand..." 201 wiped the sweat from 277's brow, shavings clinging to her fingers.

"You said that I was next... that my zulfiqar would not save me this time. You knew."

"I didn't want this, 277. I would never have done it..."

277 chuckled, her body enveloped in the fragrant wood shavings, blood from her side seeping through the curls, matting them together. "I would have expired you, it's true."

"I will venerate you," said 201.

277, gripped her arm, pulling 201 closer. "No! Venerate me by finishing this. We need you. They need you. Don't fail us."

"I will do what needs to be done. I'm so sorry, 277." She glanced at Reno, who remained motionless, his eyes revealing nothing. When she looked down she found 277 staring up at her, eyes blank, mouth open.

The gongs sounded the end of the fight. A single feathery shaving clung to her index finger, quivering in her vision as she steadied her hand to peer at the crowd through the lights. She lifted her head on reflex, pacing the ring, arms raised to the crowd in victory, her blade soaked with her companion's blood.

She smiled at the Officers, remembering her words from that day in the ration room, for tonight they held a different meaning.

You're all dead already. You just don't know it yet.

She turned to Reno, to Titan, then back to Reno, smile fixed firmly in place. They stared back at 201, eyes wide, faces pale under the lights of the Epsilon Games Ring.

26

201 sat, perched on a chair in her quarters at Epsilon, resting her head in her hands. The door sucked open to reveal Titan and Reno.

"What do you want?" she whispered. She stared at the wall, clenching her jaw.

"201," said Reno. "Look at me."

201 looked up at Reno, her reddened eyes staring through him. "What do you wish to say, Reno? What could you possibly say that would make things any different?" She laughed to herself, shaking her head.

She kicked her chair out of the way, standing to face him. "I expired my companion for nothing more than the entertainment of those Officers. Get out."

"Not tonight. Not now," said Titan.

201 stood, clenching her fists to stop her hands from shaking. She wiped her eyes, blowing out a breath.

"What did they do to her?" she said, her voice rough. "Her eyes... she was no longer there. She spoke only of her service to FERTS and she was strong, much stronger than before. What did they do to her?" she raised her voice, pacing the room.

"Keep your voice down, 201." Reno glanced at Titan, then at the door as it sucked open once more.

Officer Ryan stood in the doorway, leaning against the frame. His eyes trailed over 201 in her Epsilon jumpsuit, a smirk crossing his face. 201 stiffened, freezing in place.

"She's busy, Officer Ryan!" shouted Reno.

"Yes, it seems that our Epsilon champion is popular tonight. But what is it that you were all doing in here?" he asked, refusing to move from his position at the door.

201 lunged forward, grasping Titan's face in both hands. She kissed him with ferocity, pushing him to the bed.

"Oh," said Officer Ryan. "Perhaps another time." He backed away. "Do not forget, 201."

201 looked up from the bed, a seductive smile firmly in place. "I will visit you, Officer Ryan. You can be sure of that."

The door sucked shut, signaling Officer Ryan's departure.

201 backed away, leaving a bemused looking Titan on the bed, hair ruffled. She turned, kicking the chair in frustration, letting out a curse.

"He's gone," muttered Reno.

201 slumped to the floor, pulling her knees to her chin. "Something is wrong with all of this."

"I agree," said Reno, his eyes remaining fixed on the door. "Titan?"

Titan sat up, running a hand through his hair. "Er..." He glanced around the room, eyes fixing on 201.

"First me, then 277. Is that a coincidence, do you think?" 201 asked, looking up at Reno.

"Wait," said Titan. "You said you would visit Officer Ryan. After what he did to you. Have you lost your senses?"

201 looked over at Titan. "I do not think he understands what I meant." A slow smile crept across her features, a smile that did not reach her eyes.

"Focus, 201," said Reno. "You said first you, then 277. What are you thinking?"

"You know that there is something wrong with the wheel, with the Fighter selection. They have fixed the result to remove us. I believe that 263 is next." She narrowed her eyes at Reno. "Maybe then it will be you."

"No, that can't be right," said Titan. "They wouldn't do that, it makes no sense. It could simply be a coincidence."

"You believe this, 201? What is your reasoning?" asked Reno.

"Because they will finish what they began back at the camp. They will eliminate us, one by one. You know the orders that were given. You also know that we were not meant to return. It was my mistake to think that they would not continue once we were back within the safety and protection of FERTS." She spat out the last words, a look of displeasure on her face. She rose to her feet, pacing the room. "Pinnacle Officer Cerberus is not to be underestimated."

"How did you come to this... understanding?" asked Reno. "Did you dream this?"

"No! You know that I cannot see what once was clear to me. No, this is mere deduction. You saw Games Operator Farrenlowe tonight, and I expect you saw the wheel?" Reno nodded his head. "I thought so. Perhaps there is a reason the Officers' duties are separated in this way. I would not have expected you to act as High Training Room Officer had you known the truth. But when did you find out this information? Exactly how long have you known this? Answer me!" Reno stiffened, rising to his feet.

"I did not betray you, 201. Remember that." Reno left the room, door sucking shut behind him.

"Reno..." 201 called after him but he was gone.

Titan put his hand on 201's shoulder. "Why did you kiss me?"

"To make Officer Ryan leave," said 201. "He was suspicious. It was my first thought."

"Are you saying you did not want to?" He moved closer.

201 turned to face him, placing a hand on his chest. She pushed gently, backing him towards the door. "No, I am not saying that. I am not saying that at all. But this is not the time. One mistake and it will not matter whether I wish to kiss you or not. We must focus, Titan. You have your duties and I have mine. Now is not the time."

"Now is not the time. Right. So later?" Titan grinned at her, raising an eyebrow.

201's smile disappeared. "What if there is no later because of what we speak of now? Do not think of this, not now. We must focus on the plan and what we are fighting for. Later is for later." She gave him a final push, the door sucking open and closed behind him.

201 leaned against the wall, her breathing shallow. She touched her lips, huffing out a breath. She strode to the doorframe, gripping the top and hoisting herself into the air.

"One," she said, commencing the count for her nightly drills.

27

The next evening in the rations room, 201 sat across from 263, trying to catch her attention. 263 kept her head down, ignoring 201's attempts. She stared at her regulation protein, barely touching a single bite.

201 exhaled, pushing her own tray to the side. "263..."

263 looked up, meeting 201's eyes. "You expired my companion, 201. I do not wish to speak with you." Another Epsilon Fighter placed a hand on 263's shoulder, whispering to her.

One of the Epsilon Fighters cleared her throat to speak. "Fellow Fighters, Epsilon Internees. We will venerate 277 this night. She fought bravely and fell as a champion of FERTS in the Epsilon Games Ring." The table was silent for a moment, the Internees focused in veneration of 277.

201 stared down at her hands, clasped together on the table. She resisted the urge to speak out in the silence, remembering her promise to her companion. 277 had not wished to be venerated in this way, yet 201 had given her word to venerate her, and this was the way that 263 and the other Epsilon Internees had always venerated their fallen Fighters. 201 would

remain silent, no matter how much she disagreed with what she considered a futile ritual. She would remain silent for 277 and 263, not for FERTS itself.

After a time, the conversation resumed.

"263," she whispered. "You must listen. I can help you. I know what to do now. The Implant Markers..."

263 stood, her uneaten tray clattering to the table. She turned to address the rest of the Epsilon Internees. "I suggest we venerate the newest champion of the Epsilon Games! Let us venerate our newest spatha champion, Epsilon Fighter, 201!" The rest of the tables erupted into applause, countless Epsilon Internees making their way to 201 to pat her on the back, her shoulder, speaking words of veneration and encouragement to the latest addition to the Epsilon Fight pool.

201 attempted to stand, watching the figure of 263 depart through the doors to the ration room. She tried to push through the crowd but was stopped on numerous occasions to hear of her bravery and cunning in the ring against 277. She stopped amongst the gathered crowd, shoulders slumping. She smiled and nodded, accepting the words of veneration as she was jostled left and right by the well-wishers of Epsilon. 201 kept smiling, waiting for her moment to depart and find Reno. It was almost time.

28

Reno entered the hallway at 19:01 carrying a stack of weapons in a leather satchel. He glanced around over his shoulder to make sure he had not been followed.

"You're late." The sound of 201's voice came from one of the darkened doorways of Epsilon.

"You're lucky I'm here at all. I had to break away from the Officers party. They will head for the cider stores, then most likely back to their quarters, with or without a Vassal."

201 held out her hand from the shadows.

"I'm sorry, that's all I know. They are not required to be anywhere at this time. You will have to use your judgement." He lifted 201's bastard sword from the satchel, handing it over handle-first. "It's sheathed, but you knew that. Are you ready?"

"No," said 201.

"Good. That means you're ready to fail. That's good."

"Maybe I will fail. This is what must be done." 201 slipped the bastard sword through the neck of her jumpsuit, fastening it against her underwear. The handle dug into her hip until she shimmied it out of the way.

"You know you don't need to do this, don't you?"

"Yes, I do. But you are wrong in what you say. What must be done... it must be done from the inside."

"I hope..." Reno began.

"This is it," said 201. She tapped her hip and flexed her ankle, ensuring her sword and bone dagger were secured in place. "The plan has changed. I can no longer see. We have nothing but our ordinary senses to influence the outcome."

"Yes. You're on your own now. I wish you good fortune."

"Luck has nothing to do with this. Just as it is with the Epsilon Chance Wheel. Things are decided, even before we begin. Do not wish me good fortune."

Reno stepped closer to the doorway, peering in at 201's face. "Then I hope this is not the last time I see you."

"Thank you, Reno. I care for you." 201 smiled as Reno turned to leave.

"Reno, wait. There is something I still do not understand. You could have... no, you should have expired me when you found me. You didn't do that."

Reno shook his head. "It doesn't matter now."

"No. It does matter. You didn't expire me, you pretended to believe what I said about the mercenaries, and kept your real thoughts to yourself. You allowed me to lead you when you did not fully believe in my words. In Lina's cabin, you were going to say something. You said you thought I *was* something. What did you mean?"

Reno blew out a breath. "I thought that maybe... I thought you might be her, my little one. But you were not mine. I know that now. The timing was wrong. Besides..." Reno stared at the wall, lost in thought.

201 studied his face. "You saw Alpha Field. You know. Somehow you know what really happened to her. That's how you know she is not me. You saw something..."

"It doesn't change how I feel. Perhaps there will be time, later."

201 reached out, placing a hand on Reno's shoulder and squeezing tight.

Reno choked out a laugh, turning his head.

"Don't start caring now, Reno. It doesn't suit you."

"Go on. Get out of here. I'll keep watch until you leave."

201 gave Reno's shoulder a pat, heading down the hallway with a walk that lilted slightly to the left. Reno leaned against the wall, checking his surrounds in his peripheral vision. He watched 201 depart, smirking at her bastard sword–induced walk. His smile faded with thoughts of tomorrow. He tried not to think of where she would be going and what she would face once she arrived.

29

201 awoke to find a message poking from the slot in her quarters at Epsilon. She blinked, looking at the letters, waiting for her eyes to focus on the words.

Her eyes widened as she leapt from the coverings and rushed to ready herself for line check.

When she stood in the line of Internees, she noticed a fellow Epsilon Internee pulling a message from her pocket and looking it over. Another tucked her message in her top pocket. One of the Internees waited until the end of line check to return to her quarters, coming out with a crumpled piece of paper.

201 kept her hands in her pockets, digging her fingernails into her palms.

It's time. Tonight. It's time.

Later that evening, after night rations, 201 stood before her presentation mirror, pulling her hair back from her face. She plaited the strands in a loose braid that curled around her shoulder.

With her hair no longer falling over her eyes, she gripped the doorframe in her quarters at Epsilon, hoisting herself up, moving her awareness through the ache in her fingers, her wrists, the strain in her knuckles, focusing the pain to block out everything but the sound of her breathing.

You can't ignore me forever, 201. I see what you are doing and it's pointless. What I created will always remain. Things will always be this way, the quicker you get used to the idea, the happier you will become.

201 ignored the voice of Pinnacle Officer Wilcox. She crouched in the doorway, stretching her arms above her head and rotating her shoulders. She lifted her body, pushing her arms against the sides of the doorframe, inching her way to the top. She had managed to incorporate more and more variations into her routine each day, continually improving her drills. There was always something new to include, something extra to learn. Once a routine was mastered, a new challenge needed to be introduced. But now there was no more time. The plan was set now, and it was time to move.

She remembered Reno's words.

You can never stop learning, 201. Once you stop, once you decide that you know all there is to know will be the very moment that you fail. Remember 201. Never stop learning.

Her muscle mass had increased since returning to the gym but her own quarters were peaceful, more reflective. She needed time to regroup, time to herself, free from distractions, free from...

Talk to me, 201. You are all I can see. Surely you must be dejected at your muscle-bound appearance.

201 jolted at the unwelcome sound of Pinnacle Officer Wilcox's voice.

You are in need of guidance, that much is clear. You were so much more delicate, so much more attractive when you were a Vassal. Still, I suppose it is all you can hope for at this point, nearly over limit, scarred and muscled as you are. No longer pleasing to the discerning eye. Your prospects are narrowing for any kind of promotion, even for a Circuit as lowly as Epsilon. The clock is ticking, 201.

She readjusted her grip on the doorframe, pushing herself to the top and tapping the frame to signal the completion of the routine.

At least do me the courtesy of speaking to me. Would it be so difficult for you to speak a few words to your former Pinnacle Officer?

201 dropped to the ground in a crouch, hissing out a breath.

"If I could have," she said to the empty room, "I would have expired you twice."

For once, Wilcox was silent.

201 sat cross-legged in her quarters at Epsilon. She took the piece of rock from her jumpsuit, scratching a mark into the stone floor. She edged outwards, scratching and gouging until the symbol was completed. She sat within the symbol, thinking of the place on the rock where she had first seen it. She imagined her mind as the thread, the journey of her consciousness from outside her body, slowly making its way within. She followed the path of the symbol in her vision, tracing it with her mind, bringing her awareness closer, ever closer inwards until her mind became still and clear.

Help me. I need assistance.

Her muscles ached but she ignored them. She measured her breaths, counting to nine as she breathed in, holding the breath for a nine count, and breathing out in a slow hiss until she reached the count of nine.

The room dissolved into blackness. Points of light peeked out from the corners of the room, shining down on 201's face. The dust of Akecheta hung in the air, dancing and weaving along the shards of light. 201 felt them then, the presence of the gathered women from ancient times, their minds linking together to form a layer of protection between 201 and the influence of Pinnacle Officer Wilcox.

Call on us, 201. We will breach the walls so you can see.

201 gathered all her strength to call on the symbol in her mind, she called to the wise ones, to Beth, to join together against the barriers created by Pinnacle Officer Wilcox.

You are one of us, 201. We may be gone but our essence will remain for all time. Call on us, commune with us and we will help you. You will see what you need to see.

The symbol glowed in her mind, the collective power of the wise ones joining, growing, becoming stronger. 201's mind hummed with the growing awareness of her allies. She could almost see them, the wise ones, gathered around her, hands outstretched at the edges of the symbol. She felt the presence of Beth hovering above the gathering, her essence becoming firmer, more solid.

201 jolted as the barrier broke, images flooding through her mind. She saw Raf and Cal, leading the others on a journey, she saw Beth smiling, arms outstretched. She saw the Internees gathered in Zeta Circuit, pacing, sobbing.

She saw Titan, his face etched with concern, arms reaching out to her. She saw Reno, polishing a blade, cuts marring his fingers, a smile on his face, but most of all she saw the Officers. She saw their positions, their essence glowing in the layout of FERTS, the map becoming clearer, opening out to layers in her vision, the pieces fitting together all at once.

The Circuits appeared, highlighting the position of the tower, the furnace, the rations store. The images glowed green in her mind, lines stretching out from her awareness, mapping out her route.

She knew what she had to do.

201 focused her mind on the Implant Markers of the Internees. They glowed a dull green, encased in a ring of orange. They dotted their way through the facility as 201's mind made its way through the hallways of Beta, Omega, Kappa, Epsilon and Zeta.

The Internee markers were gathered together, tightly packed within Zeta Circuit. They bumped against each other, pushing away but there was nowhere to go.

It's nearly full. It's almost time.

Some of the markers were clustered with other markers, as if they were fused together.

Little ones. There are little ones in there!

Her mind spiraled to reveal a control room, a Guard Officer on duty, hand toying with a lever. A smirk crossed his face.

Cries emanated from the other side of the heavy door.

"Shut up in there or I pull it early," he called out.

The cries subsided.

The Guard Officer chuckled to himself, fingers swirling patterns on the ball of the lever. "Soon, soon your time will come." He kicked back from the lever, chuckling.

"Soon!" he shouted.

A muffled sob was the only reply.

30

The door to 201's quarters sucked open to reveal Officer Ryan. He folded his arms, glaring at 201.

"You said you would come to visit me in my quarters. I grow tired of waiting," he said. "Now strip."

201's eyes blinked open. She looked up from her spot on the floor, legs crossed atop the symbol.

"What is this?" asked Officer Ryan. "You have broken regulation. I will report you for defacing your quarters."

"Oh, Officer Ryan," said 201, pushing herself to her feet. "It is nothing, I grew tired of these dull floors."

"If you were bored, you should have come to me as you promised."

201 moved out of his way. "Well?" she said, gesturing to the bed. Officer Ryan removed his uniform, stretching himself out on the bed, hands behind his head.

She left for the bathroom, closing the door behind her.

"Where do you think you are going, 201? Don't make me come in there and get you!"

"Fear not, Officer Ryan, I am merely getting ready." 201 removed her jumpsuit, folding it next to the bath. She unhooked the metal strip, unwinding it from her body and hooking it beneath a towel. She rubbed her shoulder, kneading the marks until they faded. She stood before the mirror, staring at her own panicked eyes. 201 took a deep breath, moving her boots and arranging them beneath her uniform.

She stared at her reflection, her gaze darting to the washing slot and back to her own panicked eyes. Could she hide? Escape was possible, perhaps for a time, but Officer Ryan would raise the alarm. All would be lost. She blinked at her reflection, a calm seeping through her body.

There was no other choice.

"201! I grow tired of waiting. This is your last warning before I come in and..."

The door opened to reveal 201. She stood naked before Officer Ryan, hands clasped behind her back. He looked up from the bed, his lips pursed in a tight line.

"Does my appearance please you, Officer?"

The corner of Officer Ryan's mouth turned up in a sneer. "Adequate," he said, raking his eyes over her form. "You are scarred." He gestured to her shoulder. "This displeases me."

"I was taken by mercenaries, didn't you hear?" 201 said, glancing down at her wound where a jagged welt had formed. The edges of the skin had closed but it was prominent, roped and twisted. She supposed it always would be this way. 201 shrugged, meeting

Officer Ryan's eye. "Are you ready?" she asked, moving closer to the bed.

"You take too long, 201. I remember you well from last time. I look forward to this."

"So do I," said 201. She knelt on the bed, crawling towards him. "I remember you too."

Officer Ryan linked his fingers behind his head, blowing out a breath. "Finally," he said, as he felt 201 moving towards him.

His eyes widened as he felt the cool blade of the bone dagger pierce his chest. He found 201 above him, blade flashing in her hand as she brought it down again, and again and again. Officer Ryan struggled, the strength seeping from his body. All he could hear was 201's voice as she brought the blade down in an arc, blood slinging from the edge and spattering against the wall.

"I remember you," she murmured. "You like to make it hurt." She brought the blade down again, slashing across his midsection. She edged closer, straddling his stomach, looking down into his eyes, hand gripping his throat. "Does it hurt?" She slashed across his arm, eyes wild. "Does it hurt now?" she shouted, blood dripping from her hair to the white sheets below.

Officer Ryan could not answer.

201 bathed in regulation order for the last time, making sure to wash the last traces of Officer Ryan from her body. She dried herself, stepping into her clean jumpsuit. She plaited her hair, staring at her presentation mirror. Her hands shook but she ignored

them, concentrating on the image before her. Her eyes were still wild, tears pricking at the corners. She blinked them back, taking a deep breath. She reached under the bed for the metal tin, jolting as her hand touched the fading warmth of Officer Ryan's arm, wrapped in the coverings from her bed.

She settled at her mirror, prising open the lid and dipping her fingers inside. She coated her hands with the ash gathered from the remains of the outer cabins at the camp. Swiping her fingers across her face, she smeared the ash across her forehead, down her nose and across her cheeks, watching as the face in her presentation mirror became pale, her olive skin covered by the remnants of her former home.

You came to us, Officers, dressed as mercenaries. Now I come, dressed as an Internee, and I will bring Akecheta to you. I will bring Zeta Circuit to you.

She stared at her reflection, eyes blinking from the strange, powdered visage. She did not recognize the voice in her mind, though she knew it was her own.

Be ready, Officers, for I am coming for you.

31

Later that evening, Titan stood at the door of the control booth, hand poised at the door. A hand came down on his shoulder and he jolted, turning to find 201 behind him.

"You startled me," he said, studying her face. "Wow. You look... frightening."

201 nodded, traces of ash falling to the ground. She stared at the door, refusing to meet Titan's gaze.

"There's nobody inside," he said, pushing the door open. "201? Say something."

"No, there is nobody here. Not yet," said 201. "I received this through the slot earlier this morning. You were successful in sending out the message... to me at least," she said, unfolding the crumpled paper from her pocket. "Now let's hope this works."

Ten minutes later, they heard the sound of an Officer stepping through the door. Titan looked over at 201, eyes wide.

201 kept her breath shallow, staring at the boots of the Officer, ignoring the crick in her neck from wedging herself in such an uncomfortable position. She reached for her boot, edging the bone dagger into her grip.

The Officer turned away from them, muttering to himself. 201 ducked from under the desk, rising up, clamping her hand over the Officer's mouth and slicing from one side of his neck to the other. She kept her hand tight against his lips, muffling the startled shouts vibrating against her palm. 201 pulled the Officer to the ground, waiting for the sounds to cease. She opened a storage closet, pushing the Officer's body inside.

It was only then that she realized that Titan had not moved.

201 pushed the storage door shut, wedging the Officer inside. She pushed a few more times before the lock finally caught and held.

"Some help would be useful, Titan," she muttered, brushing her hands on her Epsilon jumpsuit, the stains blending with the red of the fabric.

Titan looked over at the storage closet, then back to 201. "You didn't have to expire him!"

201 rubbed her hand on her sleeve, cleaning between her fingers before the blood could dry and become crusted.

"I didn't have to expire him, you say?" She grabbed a rag from the floor, cleaning the handles of the closet. "Perhaps I should have given him a warning then, so he could report back to the Pinnacle Officer."

"I didn't mean..."

"No, perhaps we could have waited here for the guard Officers to throw us both in Zeta Circuit. Or better still, we could wait for the Pinnacle Officer himself. Perhaps we could explain to him what we are doing here!" She hissed out the words, keeping her voice low.

"It's just... does this not frighten you? Do you wish to expire another? How could you just..."

201 stepped closer to Titan, meeting his eyes. "I will tell you how I do what I do. I cannot allow myself to feel too much here, Titan. Not for anything. Or anyone."

Titan flinched, but did not blink.

"I had a choice. One Officer for all of them down there. What did you think I would do? The Officers think nothing of expiring one or many of us. Why does this surprise you?"

Titan was silent for a moment. "Aren't you afraid you will become like them?"

201 huffed out a laugh. "I will tell you something, Titan. Out there, I was someone else, someone I wanted to be. Now I must adapt to suit my environment. Or as Reno described it, I must be *versatile*. We all must do this, including you, or all is lost. Right now, I feel nothing. Nothing at all. If there is something at the end of this, I do not know what I will feel. But I cannot risk this, not now. If I fail, we all fail, and I will not let that happen."

"I won't let you fail, 201. Neither will Reno or 263," he said.

"You control nothing now. We control nothing. I wonder if we ever did. You have already risked too much for this," she said, turning away from him.

"Wait," said Titan. "Look at me." 201 reluctantly met his eyes.

"You're going after him, aren't you?"

"Who?" said 201, feigning ignorance.

"I know that look. It is the same look you gave me the night you expired Pinnacle Officer Wilcox. Now you wish to go after Officer Morton. I know you think it will help you, but it won't. And it won't help the rest of the Internees."

"No, you don't understand Titan. It helps. It helps a lot. Officer Ryan will not hurt another Internee, not now." 201 clenched her fists to stop them from shaking. "There is still time. I must make sure that the same is true for Officer Morton."

"And then what? You cannot expire all who have wronged you! Think about what you are doing. Your eyes... they speak of revenge. You cannot give in to this. It is your mind that got us this far and we need your focus to get us out of this."

"I must make sure that he will not do it again," said 201.

"No, 201. You know that is not the way. We stick to the plan, for them, not for us. Officer Morton can wait. Do you think you are the only one he has wronged?"

201 sucked in a breath.

"I think you will find he has more enemies than you think. Do what you need to do, but do not divert from the plan. They need you. I need... I need you to focus, to keep your mind clear."

"I will stick to the plan, but I cannot do all that you ask. It is out of our control now." She checked her timepiece. "I must meet Reno soon. You know what to do. I care for you Titan, you know this. When I leave, make sure... just keep yourself safe."

A flash of movement caught her eye from below.

Titan and 201 peered down from the booth to find lines of Internees from Beta, Omega, Kappa and Epsilon filing into the presentation room.

The message.

"Look. You did it, Titan," 201 whispered. "It worked." 201 sat at the console, pulling another chair close to her own.

Titan sat at the controls, readying the equipment. "It's almost time," he said. "I hope this works."

32

Internees from Beta and Omega filed into the presentation room, followed by Internees from Epsilon and Kappa Circuit. The presentation room filled quickly, forcing the Internees to stand in the aisles and press themselves against the walls at the sides and the back of the room. Confused murmurings rose up in pockets, Internees gathering together in groups, trying to ascertain the nature of their gathering. It was unusual for all Circuits to gather for a presentation evening, in fact many of them wondered if it had ever happened before. Yet each had received instructions to attend the Pinnacle Officer's presentation, following a specific route to the presentation room. Each Internee had dutifully attended as was specified in regulation.

"Why must we share the presentation room with Epsilon and Kappa?" asked an Omega Vassal. "Presentations are for Vassals only. They have no hope of becoming Vassals. This is so strange to me, I have never seen this before."

A Beta Internee stared at the gathering of Kappa Internees at the back of the room. "I have never seen a Kappa Internee before now. Orange is not very becoming, wouldn't you agree?" she said to her companion.

The Kappa Internees were mostly silent. They were never called upon for such prestigious events. Some stared open mouthed at the rich drapery and the burnished metal of the FERTS lettering adorning the Vassal logo.

The Epsilon Internees gathered around the doorways, eyes flicking around the room, taking in the surroundings. One of them turned to 263. "You know why we're here, don't you? It has something to do with 201, your new companion."

263 stared ahead, allowing her peripheral vision to take in the movement of the Internees as they settled into their seats. The Omega and Beta Internees sat at the front of the presentation room, allowing little room for the other Internees to take up the seats behind them.

"263, it's true isn't it? You know why we're here. You have changed, ever since you left to attack the rogue camp. You hardly speak of it anymore, yet when you do, your words seem strange to me. What happened at the camp? What has changed in you? Why are we here?"

263 turned to her companion, a hint of a smile on her face. "Too many questions. You will see soon enough."

The lights dimmed, fingers of light piercing through the darkness as the presentation began. Instead of the expected sight of Pinnacle Officer Cerberus, the Internees were confronted with the image of High Training Officer Reno, dressed in his usual black attire, a tan leather breastplate slung across his chest.

"As you can see, I am not the Pinnacle Officer. We do not have much time. I need you to listen to me as if this was your most important fight at Epsilon, your most prestigious Vassal presentation. This is your most important test, and one I trust you will treat with reverence."

Excited chatter rose up among the gathered Internees.

"This is something that will come as a great shock, as it was when the truth was revealed to me..." Reno took a sharp breath. "Your Pinnacle Officer is deceiving you." The figure of Reno turned to the side, addressing each of the Internees with his eyes. "There are no mercenaries waiting for you outside FERTS, nor have there ever been. They are merely Officers in disguise, designed to keep you inside. It is a method the Pinnacle Officer designed to keep you here within these walls."

A gasp rose up from the crowd.

"Internees of Beta, of Omega. There is no Alpha Field. No reward for your service to FERTS."

"What?" cried a voice from the crowd. "That is impossible!"

Reno continued on, his image flickering. "Alpha Field and Zeta Circuit are one and the same. You will be expired either way. Understand this and you may have a chance at survival."

"What is he talking about? This is treason!" shouted another voice from the crowd.

"Internees of Epsilon. Your veneration is nothing but empty words. You will all join the Internees of Zeta Circuit in the end. You are merely a distraction, a form of entertainment for the Officers. You are not venerated in their eyes. You are disposable. When you are expired, it means nothing to them."

"This cannot be," said another. "I do not believe it."

"Internees of Kappa. You will be relegated to Zeta Circuit as soon as you tire at your duties. What you do not understand is that your wood, the wood that you harvest and chop, is the very wood that will burn you in Zeta Circuit when you are too weak to continue your work."

"No, no," murmured a voice, choking back a sob.

"And Zeta Circuit, the ones you are taught to despise. The rejected, the defective, the unwanted... they are you... and you are them. There is no difference between you, whether you are a birther, a Vassal, a worker or a Fighter, you are all headed for the pit, sooner or later. Where do you think the 26Y Internees have gone? Where do you think you will go when it is time?"

Commotion broke out, a scuffle near the doors. Titan looked at 201, concern etched on his face. 201 watched the chaos below, hoping that the doors would hold until the end of the presentation.

"The truth was revealed to me by an Internee. Her name is Beth 259201."

201 reached out, taking hold of Titan's hand, eyes fixed on the screen. He looked at her from the corner of his eye, squeezing her hand.

"Traitor!" called a voice from the crowd. The Internees glanced around, trying to pinpoint the location of 201. 201 flinched, focusing her eyes on the screen.

One of the Epsilon Fighters took at step in the direction of the doors, a sneer on her face.

"Stop," said 263 flinging out her arm to halt her exit. "Hear what Officer Reno has to say."

"This is against regulation. He has betrayed the Pinnacle Officer," she replied, clenching her teeth. "You have betrayed the Pinnacle Officer."

"Please," said 263. "Just wait."

"Find the traitor!" called another voice.

201 looked over at Titan. "They cannot see me up here?" Titan shook his head. "Come on, come on," she muttered, releasing his hand. "This is taking too long. I must meet with Reno but I need to see this. Don't lose them, Titan. This is our only chance."

Titan fumbled with the controls, pressing another button.

"Find her!" shouted another. The crowd began to move towards the exits, the mass of jumpsuits winding and pushing against itself, edging closer to the doors.

The voice of Pinnacle Officer Cerberus came over the speaker.

"See the Vassals as they care for their Sires." The crowd halted at the sound of their Pinnacle Officer's voice. Each of the Internees turned, edging around each other to face the presentation screen, necks craning for a better view.

"See their joyous faces as they tend to their beloved Sires."

The beauty of Alpha Field spread out before them. They marveled at endless miles of green fields featuring Vassals leading their Sires to gather, to mingle and to congregate for activities of leisure.

The crowd sighed, the theta metronome pulsing through their minds. They stood, transfixed at the beauty on the screen as the images flickered and changed. The tranquility of Alpha Field washed over them as they gazed on the hard-won reward they had been promised for their tireless service to FERTS.

"The Vassals are fulfilled. Complete." The images flickered and switched to another location, one that did not fit with the beauty of the pictures on the screen.

One of the Internees sucked in a breath. Another made a choking sound.

The picture widened to reveal more of the scenery, guiding the Internees closer to the presentation screen. The frames flickered and moved through a dense forest, edging towards the lip of a dark chasm.

201 held her breath, watching the screen.

"See the pride in their faces," said the voice of Pinnacle Officer Cerberus. The screen trailed along the edge of the pit, discarded pieces of charred bone poking from the earth.

The remains of the Internees were piled together in a tangled heap. The shreds of Internee jumpsuits and clumps of hair lay interspersed amongst countless piles of insignia.

One of the insignia came into view, resting at the top of the pile. A charred hand raised from the tangle of bones, another hand protectively covering a smaller form, the bones of a tiny hand gripping the larger ribcage.

"236!" one of the Beta Internees cried. "But 236 was a birther Vassal! She was promoted to Alpha Field! What is the meaning of this?" She stepped forward, stretching her hand towards the presentation screen.

"There must be some mistake. This cannot be..." said another voice.

The screen panned over the pit, revealing a multitude of bones, charred skulls and cooked flesh teeming with voracious insects.

"See how the Vassals are venerated," said the soothing voice of Pinnacle Officer Cerberus.

The shot widened, showing the vastness of the pit, bones upon bones, piled in careless layers. The vision panned back, unable to fit the edges of the pit within the confines of the screen.

"Alpha Field. Your reward for your tireless service to FERTS." The Pinnacle Officer's voice cut through the silence as the Internees stared at the screen. Some wept, some clenched their fists and stepped towards the screen. Some whispered to themselves, shaking their heads.

"We will now give thanks to Pinnacle Officer Cerberus and FERTS, for our provision and protection against those who would strike against our Fighters, our Vassals and our Internees." The voice washed over the assembled crowd, the words of the FERTS Requital hanging in the silence of the presentation room.

There was no response.

33

201 slipped out of the control booth, meeting up with Reno at the designated location. Together, 201 and Reno hurried through the hallways, spotting two guard Officers at the end of Beta Circuit. The first guard Officer stepped forward, blocking their path.

"Stop. Why are you here, Officer Reno? And what is an Epsilon Internee doing in Beta Circuit?"

Reno stopped before them, out of breath. "There's been a security breach, it's that way. I had to come and alert you."

The first guard Officer reached for his radio. "And what about..." He gestured to 201.

"She was... keeping me company when the alert came." 201 hid her surprise, keeping her expression blank.

Reno reached for the radio. "Here, let me." 201 took the opportunity to edge her way around the first guard Officer, rounding the second. She smiled at him, lowering her gaze.

"Can I ask you something?" She moved closer to the second guard Officer. A scowl crossed his face.

"What do you want?"

He cried out in surprise as 201 plunged the blade into his chest.

The first guard Officer turned his head, shock registering on his face. Reno dug his elbow into the Officer's throat, startling him before spearing him with his spatha.

The Officers dropped to the ground, falling between Reno and 201.

Reno looked down at the first guard Officer's face. "I'm sorry."

Confusion crossed his features as the blood drained from his body. "I don't understand."

201 bent down, unclipping the radios from the Officers and handing them to Reno.

"I know you didn't want to do that," she said.

Reno shook his head. "No, I didn't. But this has to end. It has to end now." He met 201's eyes. "Get out of here, 201. I'll join up with Titan at the meeting place. Go!"

34

The room was silent, the last words of the presentation reverberating in the air. The Internees looked to one another, unsure of what to think. One of the Beta Internees spoke up.

"Where is 201?"

263 stepped forward from the gathered group of Epsilon Internees.

"201 has already begun to carry out the plan," said 263. "But she cannot do this alone. We need to be clear, and we need to do this together." She scanned the faces before her. Some appeared confused, others bore the look of shock. But some, she noted, had a look she had not seen before on her fellow Internee's faces outside the Epsilon Games Ring. It was the look of one who was prepared to fight, no matter what the risk.

"There is a place for all of us. A camp. You will not be required to perform Vassal duties. You will not be required to serve a Vendee or an Officer. It is a place where there are no Epsilon Games, no Circuits, no regulation. It is a place where all of us can be free," said 263.

"How can this be?" asked one of the Beta Internees. "Surely we would have heard of such a place as this."

"The Officers at FERTS did not know of the camp or its location. But I have seen it. It is as real as you and me as we stand here tonight," said 263.

"Those of you who do not wish to fight, I ask that you take yourselves in groups to this point here." She gestured to a spot on the map. "You must remain here until we give you the signal to come out." A number of the Internees filed out, heading for the designated safe point, deep within the confines of the facility. 263 surveyed the remaining Internees.

"The rest of you are standing here because you wish to fight. I will not pretend that this will be without risk. Those of you who wish to leave may join the others."

"We wish to fight!" said one. She was joined by others, affirming their decision as they stood together.

When she had finished running through the plan, the Internees who were prepared to fight stepped forward. 263 directed them to the presentation store room, where Reno had transferred the weapons from the Epsilon weapons store.

"Your most important task is to keep your movements quiet. Contain any damage and keep to the shadows. Officers Reno, Titan and Harold are not to be harmed. There may be others but you must use your own judgement in the matter. There are some who will wish to leave unharmed. There will be others who will do whatever is necessary in order to alert the

Pinnacle Officer. This must not happen. A lot depends on this."

263 went through the plan again until it was clear that the rest of the Internees understood.

"Now go," she said. "I would wish you good luck but it appears even our fortunes were chosen for us before the Epsilon Chance Wheel could spin. I will hope that I will see you all again."

Each took a weapon, leaving in groups for their respective Circuits. 263 turned to her fellow Epsilon Internees. "Follow me," she said, leading the way down the hall towards Epsilon Circuit.

The Epsilon Internees waited at the corner, keeping watch on a guard Officer. He remained still for a time, watching the entrance to Epsilon. After ten minutes he began to make his way down the hallway towards their group. 263 raised a hand, putting a finger to her lips, signaling for them to remain silent. When the guard Officer rounded the corner, 263 struck with her trident, pinning the Officer against the wall, the trident piercing his body in three places. The Epsilon Internees placed him in one of the empty quarters, using a sheet from one of the beds to wipe up the drag marks.

"Never mind that," said 263, watching one of the Internees rub the sheet against the floor. She pulled it away to reveal the drips and lines that had already soaked down into the stone. "Come. There be others."

263 and the Epsilon Internees made their way down the hall, heading deeper into Epsilon Circuit.

35

Reno nudged Titan, giving him a nod. Titan squeezed his eyes shut, hissing out a breath. He unfastened the top of his uniform, and ran a hand through his hair, making it unruly. He stepped into the hallway, revealing himself to the two guard Officers. He staggered, righting himself at the last moment, one hand braced on the wall. He chuckled to himself, humming a tune.

The first guard Officer regarded him with a sneer.

"Officer Tire-ton, Sir. At your service." He snickered to himself. "Service, Sir."

"The cider hall is that way," said the second, rolling his eyes.

"Cider for me," he sang, the off-key notes muffled by his laughter.

"We'll send you to Zeta if you're not careful," said the other.

He clamped his arms around the first guard Officer, sighing in resignation. "Gimme... I'll call 'em!" He pulled the radio free, clumsily clicking at the button and missing his mark.

"This is Officer Ti-tron reporting for cider. Send Vassals!" The guard Officer tried to pull the radio free from Titan's grip. The other Officer watched the exchange, a look of disapproval on his face.

"I repeat, send Vassals." He pressed the button too hard, snapping it off. "Oop..." The guard Officer grunted, reaching for his radio again, reluctant to leave his designated post. Titan chuckled into the broken radio, pressing the spot where the button had been. "Send Vassals... and radios!" He descended into laughter. The Officers were so caught up in Titan's antics that they failed to notice the figure of Reno rising up behind them and snapping the second Officer's neck.

Titan punched the first Officer, hard enough for him to stagger back into Reno's grip. Reno clamped his hands on either side of the Officer's head, twisting his neck with a crack. Titan winced at the sound, hooking his arms under the second Officer and dragging him down the hall. Reno slung the first Officer over his shoulder and followed Titan, stowing the bodies in a vacant room, out of sight from the main hallway.

"That was pretty good. Just don't sing next time," said Reno.

"Too noisy? Do you think anyone heard?" Titan pushed the Officer through the door, securing it.

"No, not too noisy. You were surprisingly quiet. Just horrible."

"Oh, you joke? Now?" Titan shook his head.

"Just trying to stay level," said Reno.

"Well, you're not as funny as you think you are," said Titan, wiping his sweaty palms on his uniform.

"Seriously, though. How are you with all of this? You okay?"

"No," said Titan.

"At least you're not fooling yourself," said Reno. "You're like 201 in that way."

"I've never expired anyone before."

"And you still haven't. Technically."

"Do you think she'll be all right?" asked Titan, adjusting his uniform.

Reno sighed, leaning against the wall. He ran his hand over his bald head, wiping away the sweat. "I have every confidence in 201's abilities. I have tried to teach her everything I know. She is prepared as she will ever need to be."

"That doesn't answer my question," said Titan, face becoming grim.

"And I'm not going to fool either of us by saying what I cannot pretend to know. Come on."

36

201 snaked through the hallways, crouching in shadows, making her way past the various stockpile rooms that housed the Implant Markers, batteries, electrical components, soaps and various grooming items. She resisted the urge to scratch her nose, the ash beginning to itch against her skin. She breathed shallowly, attempting to ignore the stench of sweat and human waste seeping from the entrance to Zeta Circuit. The main hall cage was empty, and that meant only one thing.

Footsteps jolted her awareness, the sound emanating from the heart of Zeta Circuit.

She held her breath behind one of the store room doors as a guard Officer walked past her position. It was strange, she thought, that all the beauty products would be held in Zeta Circuit, as the Internees were unlikely to see another bar of soap once confined within these walls. She listened for the sound of steps retreating, glancing back at the boxes lining the room.

Two guard Officers stood at the entrance to Zeta Circuit, radios fastened to their belts. The radios were on standby, as regulation dictated, in order to save the power from their finite supply of batteries. The first Officer stared straight ahead. The other glanced around, bored. Soon they would have something to keep their interest as the furnace had been marked for incineration. Incineration day was the most eventful time in Zeta Circuit, and the hand-picked Officers looked forward to their duties once the time came.

A rattling sound started up, coming from a bend in the hallway, to the left of their position. The first Officer craned his head.

"You hear that?" asked the first.

"Yeah, I heard something," said the other.

A tiny clatter sounded, a mess of Implant Markers scattering across the floor, spilling out into the hallway.

"Rats?"

"Again?" The first Officer stepped forward. "I'll have to move it, in case the Pinnacle Officer sees it before he comes to inspect the incineration. It can't come soon enough, if you ask me."

The other Officer nodded, remaining in place. He watched the first Officer disappear around the corner. He thought he heard something else, but it was too muffled to tell what it was. Moments later his radio crackled at his belt. He fumbled to unhook it, listening to the sounds coming over the static.

The static hissed at him, clicking once, twice, three times.

"Hello?" he replied, pressing the transmission button.

The static continued to hiss, clicking once, twice, three times.

A lone quartz paperweight rolled out into the hallway, teetering on its axis and coming to a stop. The guard Officer moved towards the source to investigate.

He rounded the corner to find drops of blood leading to a store room. He headed for the door, standing in the shadows of the doorway, trying to make out a strange shape on the floor. It seemed large enough to be an Officer, but he couldn't understand what he was seeing. A trickle seeped out from the crumpled form, running through the cracks in the stone floor.

He took another step, reaching for his radio. A smattering of ashes drifted down from above. He watched them float and dance through the half-light, swirling around his head. He looked up to find a dark-haired Epsilon Fighter wedged at the top of the doorway, face smeared with ash, grinning down at him.

37

The Zeta Circuit Officer sat in the control room, feet resting next to the lever. Two more hours to go, he thought. Not long now.

"Shut up in there!" he called, silencing the cries behind the heavy door. He smirked, toying with the lever. "Wait until the Pinnacle Officer gets here! We're going to put on quite a show for him, don't you think?"

"Please..." came a small voice from behind the door.

"Shut up or I pull it early!" The voices fell silent.

His radio crackled, static coming in waves, growing louder.

"What? What is it?" he said, clicking the button.

"Help..." said the voice. He frowned at his radio, putting it up to his ear. The voice was so soft he could barely hear it. He thought it was one of the Officers but he couldn't be sure.

"Repeat," he said, clicking the button once more.

"...coming for you..." The voice hissed through the radio. The hairs on his arm began to tingle. The voice didn't sound like an Officer, not exactly, though it was hard to tell with all that static. He shook his head. He must have been imagining things. For a moment he had thought the voice had sounded... pleased?

A crash sounded against the door, sending him scrambling to his feet. So, the Officers wanted to play. Surely there must be better ways to relieve the boredom. Cider, the company of Vassals...

Another thump as something hit the door again. This time, with more force.

"What the..."

He left the console unattended, swinging open the door.

"Hey, that's enough!" he shouted. He peered outside, finding the hallway empty. A broken chair lay beside the door, splinters scattered at his feet.

He stepped through the door, scanning the hallway for the other Officers and examining the remains of the chair.

He stood, spine going rigid.

Something had moved behind him.

He turned to find an Epsilon Fighter standing in Zeta Circuit. He felt cool metal connect with his temple and he dropped to the ground. Looking up, he saw the face of the Epsilon Fighter, dark hair with hazel eyes, slanted like a cat's. Her face, powdered with ash, swam in and out of focus but he could tell one thing and one thing only.

She was laughing.

38

"Come." Pinnacle Officer Cerberus sat at his desk, brow creased in thought, papers spread before him. He rested his hand on the quartz paperweight, narrowing his eyes at the figure in the doorway.

"Sir." Reno's face was flushed, sweat glistening on his forehead. He sucked in a breath, his voice catching in his throat. "Sir, you must come. It's urgent."

"What is it, Reno? I am busy, as you can see." Cerberus raised an eyebrow, making no move to rise from his chair. A 15Y Internee stood in the doorway to the bathroom, fidgeting with her Beta jumpsuit. "The Vassal presentation went smoothly, I presume?" He turned to the Internee. "Go and get the bath ready. You must bathe first, in regulation order. I will tell you when it is time to come out."

The Internee nodded, shutting the door behind her.

Reno took a deep breath. "I'm sure the presentation was fine. It's not that. I..." Reno glanced at the doorway behind him. "I can't explain. You have to see this."

Cerberus sighed, pushing away from the desk. Reno backed away, turning towards the door.

"Reno," said Cerberus. "Wait."

Reno stilled in the doorway, the Pinnacle Officer's breath warming the back of his neck.

"It would be foolish for me to leave without my guard Officers, wouldn't you agree?"

Reno was silent.

"Guard Officer!" The Pinnacle Officer called, his voice echoing through the hallway. Reno forced himself not to flinch.

There was no response.

"Guard Officer!" He turned to Reno. "Where are my guard Officers, Reno?"

Officer Titan rounded the corner, heading towards them.

"Sir, your guard Officers are already dealing with the situation," said Titan, struggling to catch his breath. "Officer Reno and I will accompany you."

"What's the meaning of this, Reno? My guard Officers are to be posted at all times. This is unacceptable."

"Sir, you can tell them yourself. We must go now!" Reno gestured for the Pinnacle Officer to follow.

Cerberus glanced through the doorway. The halls were silent, devoid of movement.

"Sir!" Reno shouted. "Sir, there's no time! Come on!" Reno and Officer Titan began to run, picking up speed as they rounded the corner. Cerberus hesitated, watching his Officers depart, their footfalls sharp in the silence.

"Wait..." he said, his voice echoing in the empty hallway.

Pinnacle Officer Cerberus broke into a run.

39

Lines of Internees streamed into their respective Circuits in regulation order. A line of orange flowed into Kappa, each Internee regulation distance behind the one in front. The Internees walked without haste. On first glance, it was not apparent that the Internees walked more carefully than would be deemed necessary. If one cared to notice, perhaps their legs appeared straighter, their gait favoring one side more than the other. The Kappa Internees were quieter than the night before, but this was not unusual after a day of chopping wood with heavy axes. Often in Kappa Circuit, there was little time for conversation after the exhaustion of the day had begun to set in. The guard Officers noticed nothing unusual about the line until three of the Internees broke regulation order. The Internees gathered around the first Officer, producing their concealed spathas and expiring first one, then the other. The remaining Kappa Internees carried the bodies of the guard Officers, making their way deep into Kappa Circuit.

The Internees of Beta filed through to their quarters, smiling their presentation smiles at the Officers as they passed. One stopped, whispering to one of the Officers. Another smoothed her hand down the other guard Officer's uniform, making the necessary arrangements for the evening. When the Beta Internees and conferred Vassals retired to their quarters, the Officers made their way into the Internees' quarters, the doors sucking shut behind them.

The first Officer arrived to find a Beta Vassal sitting on the bed, dutifully smiling up at him.

"Strip," he ordered as he began to removing his uniform.

"You are impatient tonight, Officer," said the Vassal. She smoothed a lock of shiny blonde hair behind her ear. "I thought we would try something different tonight."

The guard Officer looked at her, scowling. "I am not interested. And you are still dressed. Strip. I will not ask again."

"Then turn your back, Officer. I am shy this evening." The Vassal smiled up at him, fluttering her lashes and stroking her clavicle.

The Officer laughed. "Shy? I have taken you more times than I can count, Vassal. I am not in the mood for games. I must return to my post within the hour."

The Vassal sighed, checking her nails. "Fine," she said, smiling and clenching her teeth. The Officer turned to fold his jacket over a nearby chair. The Vassal leapt from the bed, piercing the Officer's back with a bastard sword. She caught the Officer as he fell, clamping her manicured hand over his mouth.

"You will not take me again," she whispered, lowering him to the floor beside the bed. She kicked the Officer's body to the side, pulling the bastard sword free and wiping the blade clean on the sheets.

The Internees of Omega waited dutifully in their quarters. An Omega Vassal stared at the presentation mirror, smoothing her glossy dark hair over her shoulder. The door opened, an Officer stepping inside. Doors opened throughout Kappa, Epsilon, Beta and Omega. The Officers entered the rooms, doors sucking shut behind them. Time passed, yet none of the Officers returned. The halls were quiet, save for the muffled cries seeping out from behind the doors.

40

Zeta Circuit was empty when Reno, Titan and Pinnacle Officer Cerberus arrived, the stone rooms partially cloaked in darkness. The silence was unnerving, devoid of the usual sobs and wailing.

Pinnacle Officer Cerberus looked around, stepping closer to the heavy door and prising it open. The door creaked and groaned, yawning open to reveal stone floors caked with soot, a tap dripping somewhere in the distance.

"But..." Pinnacle Officer Cerberus narrowed his eyes, his brow furrowing. He turned to face Reno. "There's nothing there."

A flash of red filled his vision from above. 201 swung from the overhead pipes, her boots connecting with his cheek. He toppled off balance, swaying in the half-darkness. 201 crouched to the ground, kicking out with her leg and buckling him at the knees as he fell through the doorway.

His eyes widened in understanding, adrenaline spiking through his body. He lunged towards 201, but her bone dagger glanced his forearm. The shock of the cut was nothing compared to the realization of what was happening.

"No!" Pinnacle Officer Cerberus clutched at the doorway, his hands scrabbling for purchase. "No!"

201 kicked at his stomach, his hands losing their grip on the doorway. He toppled back, elbows breaking his fall on the hard stone floor. The door swung towards him, sealing his only remaining exit.

Pinnacle Officer Cerberus lay on the floor, watching in horror as the doorway extinguished the last sliver of remaining light.

"NO!"

201 closed the bolt from the outside, lifting the heavy metal crossbar back on its hooks, sealing Pinnacle Officer Cerberus inside.

"Reno!" Pinnacle Officer Cerberus banged with his fists, his voice muffled through the heavy door.

201 leaned against the wall, panting. Reno stood against the door, hand flat against the crossbar.

"You can't do this to me Reno! You don't have the courage!" The Pinnacle Officer's voice was thin, rasping as he shouted to be heard.

Reno stared at the door, a trickle of sweat making its way from his temple to his cheek. He glanced at 201. 201 straightened, putting her hand on Reno's shoulder, shaking her head.

"Let me out and all will be forgiven," said Pinnacle Officer Cerberus. "You will receive promotion. You won't go through with this, I know it!"

Reno turned, leaning his back on the door. "You're right, you know," said Reno, a shaky breath escaping. "I won't go through with this."

A cry of triumph sounded from the other side of the door. "So let me out!" shouted Cerberus. "We will talk about this. About your promotion. You won't be disappointed!"

"I won't go through with this," said Reno. "I won't".

He pushed away from the door, making his way past the darkened control room.

He flicked the switch, illuminating the faces of the Zeta Internees gathered inside. Their ragged jumpsuits glowed at the edges, the worn threads highlighted by the harsh lights. Hollowed eyes stared out from gaunt faces, the sharp edges of their cheekbones catching the light. Their eyes blinked back at him, tracking his movements. One of the Zeta Internees stood up, waiting for the signal, her bony hand poised above the iron lever. Another stepped forward, her emaciated body shuffling underneath her jumpsuit. She nodded at Reno.

"I won't go through with it, but they will." He nodded his head, raising his hand to the Zeta Internees as he walked away from Zeta Circuit without looking back.

"Reno! RENO!!" screamed Cerberus, the sound making its way to the control room. 201 stood before the door, hands clenched at her sides.

Titan looked over at 201 as the Zeta Internee gripped the lever. "Reno was right to leave," he said. "You don't have to be here when this happens, 201. You've done enough."

201 shook her head, feet planted firmly in place.

"No," said 201. "Go with Reno. I have to know. I have to make sure this is done. This ends now." She dug her nails into her palms and nodded at the Zeta Internee to pull the lever. "Do it."

The Zeta Internee gripped the heavy iron lever. She pulled, but her strength gave out before it could engage. She held her wrist, grimacing.

Pinnacle Officer Cerberus lifted himself from the stone floor, staring at the outline of the door. Surely Reno had heard him correctly and understood his offer of promotion. The tap dripped in the distance, splashing out of time with his ragged breaths.

"Reno? Is that you?"

"Pinnacle Officer Cerberus!" called a voice from the other side of the doorway. An Internee.

"Yes?" He moved to the doorway to hear. "Who is this?"

"Reno told me you were looking for someone. The one who expired Pinnacle Officer Wilcox." The Internee's voice filtered through the door, unfamiliar to Cerberus' ears.

"Well, come on, out with it!" snapped Cerberus, pounding the door with his fist.

"You have found her," said 201.

"What?" Cerberus' head began to swim, images swirling through his mind. He thought of the Epsilon whelp on the other side of the door and how it was that she had managed to expire Pinnacle Officer Wilcox. His vision swam with images of Wilcox on the floor of the elevator, his face pale in the lights of the backup generator, blood soaking the front of his immaculate silver uniform. He wondered how it could be that of all the possibilities, a simple Internee was the one to have expired the Pinnacle Officer. He fumbled for his radio.

How could I have been so wrong? An Internee. A common Internee!

One of the Zeta Internees reached out, grasping the lever. She gave a signal to her companion who stepped forward and placed a hand atop her own. Another Zeta Internee covered their hands with hers as the others stepped forward. And another, and another, and another. With their combined strength, they pulled the lever as one, engaging the incinerator of Zeta Circuit and dragging it to the active position.

A chill ran through Cerberus as the clunk of the furnace echoed through the stone room. A whooshing noise started up and he felt a gust ruffling his hair.

No, not that. Not that. Not like this.

He closed his eyes, hissing out a breath. So this is how it ends, he thought. She expired the Pinnacle Officer and you can do nothing about it. Now you know, and you can do nothing.

No. Not one Pinnacle Officer, but two.

Pinnacle Officer Cerberus stood in the corner of the Zeta Circuit incineration room, watching his shadow dance on the wall as the flames roared towards him. His ankles stung as his boots fused to his legs. The heat penetrated his uniform, the rows of insignia glowing brightly before dropping to the ground. Pinnacle Officer Cerberus screamed as his hair ignited, eyes boiling in their sockets. Flames licked at his neck and sucked down his throat as he gasped for air.

201 leaned against the door, stepping away as the warmth of the furnace radiated against her shoulders. The sounds of Pinnacle Officer Cerberus' cries mingled with the sounds of another voice screaming inside her head.

It was the voice of Pinnacle Officer Wilcox.

201 jolted, startled from her thoughts as the siren began to wail. The Zeta Internees froze. 201 looked back at the door, imagining what lay inside. The siren. Pinnacle Officer Cerberus had a radio. This was no coincidence.

The siren blared, filing her ears in pulses. "His radio," she muttered. "There was no time to remove it. What have I done?" She backed away from the door, the smell of burning flesh assaulting her nostrils. "Raf... the others. They're in danger. This is my fault!"

201 failed to notice that the Zeta Internees were closer now, their eyes blank, pupils dilated. She turned to face them. They smiled in unison.

"We now give thanks to Pinnacle Officer Cerberus and FERTS..." they chanted.

201 backed away from the advancing group. One of the Zeta Internees blinked, gritting her teeth and attempting to regain her composure. "201," she whispered. "Get out. Get out now. I can't stop it."

201 ran.

41

Rafaella crouched beside a rock, turning to face her companions.

"So, we're clear on the plan. Make no mistake. We don't have the element of surprise this time. This is war. We start at the entrance and make our way through until we get to Zeta Circuit. This time we leave nobody behind. Got it?" Rafaella unsheathed her saber. "Cal, you ready?"

Caltha nodded.

"You shouldn't be here, you know. Same with you, Jotha."

"I'm fine, Raf. We're fine. Let's do this," said Caltha. Bonni, Kap, Vern, Jotha and Liam gathered behind Rafaella. Behind them stood 292 and the former Internees of Zeta Circuit, all dressed in warrior attire. They had filled out since escaping Zeta Circuit, their arms well-muscled, cheeks flushed with vigor.

"I know this is hard for you, returning here. You're brave just to go through with this. If they've got that beacon up and running again, you need to stay inside the grounds. I don't need to tell you this, but... just be careful. Try to stay alive."

"We are not afraid," said one of the Zeta Internees.

"We're ready," said another.

"Right," said Rafaella. "Follow me."

Operator Linum caught a flash of movement on the monitor. A stream of Implant Markers was coming from the south east, moving towards FERTS, rather than the other way around. What was the protocol here? The beacon needed to be activated whenever an Internee's Implant Marker was spotted moving away from the facility, but surely the reverse would be true as well. He watched the markers glowing on the monitor, filing through the main entrance.

"So many..." he said.

His radio crackled, the shrill voice of Pinnacle Officer Cerberus coming through the static.

"Sound the beacon!" he shouted. His voice was muffled by a roar and a crackling sound before the radio went dead. Operator Linum stared at the radio in his hand. He clicked the button.

"Sir?"

The radio was silent. Operator Linum sighed. He flicked the protective cover away from the button and pressed it.

Rafaella, Caltha and the others burst through the entrance to FERTS, finding themselves in an empty atrium. The room was beautiful, decorated in drapes and finery, flowers placed on side tables, their petals beginning to wilt.

A roar sounded as the beacon started up, the former Zeta Internees standing in place, weapons raised. The sharp clatter of footfalls on stone echoed through the hallways leading to the main atrium.

"Stand your ground!" shouted Rafaella, awaiting the arrival of the Officers. Jotha and Caltha flanked Rafaella's position, crossbows poised, ready to fire.

The sound grew stronger, the thump of what sounded like hundreds of pairs of boots filling their ears.

Rafaella listened, her saber poised in front of her body, her other hand raised in warning.

"I don't like this," whispered Caltha. "There are too many. Unless..."

"This isn't right. There aren't that many Officers," said Rafaella. "Something's wrong here."

The stomping sound echoed through the atrium. Rafaella looked up to see the red of Epsilon, the blue of Omega, the orange of Kappa and even the white of Beta jumpsuits swarming out into the atrium. Their eyes were dark, their pupils open to reveal a horrible blankness. They snarled at the group of intruders, eyes blank, weapons raised. One of the Epsilon Fighters cried out, heading towards Rafaella.

"What the..." said Kap.

"It's 263," said Caltha.

"Fall back!" shouted Rafaella. The group edged back, heading for the doorway. "Fall back and aim to incapacitate!" They turned to find the Zeta Internees gathered at the entrance, blocking their escape.

"Get out of the way!" Rafaella shouted, charging towards them. They smiled, raising their weapons.

"This is bad. This is so bad," she muttered. "Step aside," she said, facing the Zeta Internees.

"Can't do that, Raf," said one, clutching her chest and struggling to regain control of her senses. "I don't want to fight you, but I feel I must. We must defend FERTS. I have no choice." The saber in her hand began to shake.

"Get out of the way. Please," she said. The sound of boots grew closer, the clink of weapons growing in volume.

"I don't want to do this," said Rafaella, her fist connecting with the Zeta Internee's cheekbone. She fell, toppling into the surrounding Internees. Rafaella threw another punch, Jotha and Kap pushing and hitting out against the group as they squeezed through the doors, dodging sabers and spathas.

They stumbled out through the main entrance, spilling out onto the grounds. Jotha ran to bar the door, but the Internees were already pushing through.

"Get out of there Jotha!" yelled Rafaella. "Come on, get back!" The Zeta Internees turned to face them, rising to their feet and joining the seemingly endless stream from Epsilon, Kappa, Beta and Omega.

"Get back!" shouted Caltha, edging towards the tree line.

"No!" shouted one of the Zeta Internees, feeling her movements drawing her closer to the tree line and the edge of the suspension zone. She knew she would advance, regardless of the cost. "The beacon!"

Caltha knelt, aiming her crossbow at their advancing opponents. She aimed for the lower leg, her bolt finding its mark. She aimed for the arm, making contact. When one fell, another took her place. She could see her efforts doing nothing to slow their opposition.

She grabbed her saber, rushing at the group, slashing at arms, shins, whatever she could reach. She heard Kap shouting at Rafaella behind her.

"Where are the Officers? Why are we fighting the Internees? We're supposed to be rescuing them, not fighting them! What's wrong with them?"

"I don't know, Kap!" yelled Rafaella. "Just try not to hurt them too much!"

"Don't hurt them?" He struck out at an Internee, wounding her fighting arm. "They're trying to kill us!"

"Why aren't we back at the tree line?" shouted Jotha, slashing at a Beta Internee's shin. "We're too exposed out here!"

"No! Hold your position!" ordered Rafaella, fending off an Epsilon Internee. "The Internees, they'll follow us! They won't make it past the tree line. The beacon!"

Vern hit out at a bastard sword, knocking the Kappa Internee to the ground with his fist. He glanced at the tree line and back to their position near the entrance of FERTS. He watched the Internees gaining ground, backing them towards the trees. "We're trapped!" he shouted.

42

201 ran through the halls, passing stains and drag marks, remnants of the Officers cut down by the weapons of Epsilon. She passed open doors, trails of blood snaking through the quarters of Omega. She was getting close. The clash of weapons sounded to her right. She spotted Titan and Reno, fighting back a trio of Omega Vassals, their untrained moves more precise than 201 would have expected. They turned to stare at 201, eyes swimming with darkness.

"There she is!" said one.

"The traitor!"

"Expire her!"

The Omega Vassals began to advance. Reno blocked them with his spatha, pushing them back. Titan held a trident, backing them towards the wall.

"The beacon!" shouted 201. "They can't fight against this! I have to stop it!"

"Not yet 201!" shouted Reno, keeping his attention on the Omega Vassals. "It's not secured yet!"

One of the Omega Vassals kicked out at Titan, forcing him back towards the opposing wall. His trident hit the ground beside him.

"Titan..." said 201, moving towards them.

Titan picked up his Trident, righting himself and pointing it at the Vassal's neck, backing her against the wall. "Go, 201!" he shouted.

She turned and ran for the tower, scaling the steps two at a time.

43

201 burst through the control room doors with a cry.

Operator Linum twirled around in his seat. His eyes nearly crossed staring at the tip of 201's bastard sword.

"Up. Get up and I will not harm you." Operator Linum backed away from the console, hands trembling.

"In the corner. Don't move." 201 gestured to the console. "How do you stop this?"

"Stop what?" Linum glanced around the room, eyes darting to the doorway.

"Do not play with me!" 201 shouted. "My companions are down there. I do not wish to harm you. I will ask again. How do I turn this off?"

Operator Linum's eyes swept the control room, coming to rest on 201. He pointed to the red button on the console. 201 stepped forward, flicking off the protective cover.

"I wouldn't do that if I were you, defective." 201's eyes widened, freezing at the sound of the Officer's voice.

Morton.

Her eyes darted to the doorway to find Morton towering above her. 201 lunged for the button. The blow was sharp at the side of her head, tears welling up before she collapsed to her knees, her bastard sword clattering to the ground and skidding across the floor.

Officer Morton smiled down at her. "I remember you. I remember you well." He kicked her bastard sword out of the way. "So, you're the one who has been causing all this trouble."

201 wiped the blood from her mouth, eyes darting to the console.

"I remember you too, Morton," she said.

Morton crouched before her, the breadth of his shoulders blocking her view of the exit. "Well. You don't look like much, do you? Did you do all this? You were foolish to try this against FERTS. You should never have returned here. But I'm so glad you did."

201 glanced around, looking for her weapon, some kind of distraction, anything to stop what was coming. Her eyes strayed to the console, the button out of her reach.

"I wouldn't advise that. I will not make the mistake of turning my back on you. Word is that an Internee has been causing disruptions to the morale in Epsilon Circuit. I don't suppose you know anything about that?" Morton smiled, his dark beard obscuring most of his teeth. "I know what you are thinking right now. There's no need to search for a way out of here, for there is none. Not for you, anyway."

201 focused her eyes on the button. One push and it would be over. She would be expired but Rafaella, Caltha, Titan, Reno and the rest her companions would be safe. Officer Morton followed her gaze.

"I wouldn't try that, defective. You are too clever for your own good. If you push that button I will expire you." Officer Morton tilted his head down to peer at her. "And then I will simply push it back on. You will have achieved nothing."

"Just do it." 201 raised her head, baring her neck, hands clasped at the top of her head. "I do not wish to hear you speak."

"But why, 201? We are having so much fun." Morton smiled at her, eyes narrowing. "Just like last time."

201 met Officer Morton's gaze. "I know what it is you do here. And it is not about protection. What Wilcox started, Cerberus continued. I know all about Zeta Circuit. And I know about Alpha Field. And now..." 201 nodded to the grounds outside. "So do my fellow Internees."

"I don't know about that, not that it matters anyway. All I know is you're interfering where you shouldn't. But I would like to know why you're the only one who is not affected by the beacon," said Officer Morton. "Perhaps you are more of a defective than you seem to be."

A ragged scream rose up from the grounds below, the distant clink of swords peppering the unnatural quiet of the control room. 201 flinched, her brows drawing together.

"They with you?" Morton asked, gesturing to the window. 201 looked away, focusing on the wood panels on the wall. "Yes, I thought so. Your companions, these rogues, they are losing, defective. Perhaps you do not understand who you are fighting against. The Internees are all one now, and they will defend FERTS to the last. They will fall for FERTS, and will be proud to do so."

"You lie," said 201.

Officer Morton suppressed a grin as the siren blared on. "Well, that's what Pinnacle Officer Cerberus told me."

201 clenched her fists. "They will merely do what the Implant Markers dictate. And they will do it for the Pinnacle Officer only because they have been forced to do so. You cannot hide the truth. Not anymore."

He shrugged, glancing at the button, then over to the dial beside it on the console. "If they defect, I press the one that ends it." He moved away to reveal another button, encased in a larger casing. He raised an eyebrow. "You think you know everything but you didn't know about this one, did you?" He smiled. "One push and pfft." He mimed an explosion with his hands. "All gone. The charge will go straight to their hearts. It would be over in moments."

"You wouldn't." 201 gritted her teeth, hiding the wave of shock that ran through her body. She forced a smile. "FERTS would be finished. What would you do for Vassals?"

"There are still some Vassals in the townships. We would do what we did in the beginning."

"You would become mercenaries once more and take them. Start again," 201 muttered.

Officer Morton's eyes widened.

"How did... well, I suppose you know an awful lot for an Internee. But you can say goodbye to your rogue companions down there. They are no match for the beacon. Our Internees know nothing now but how to expire a threat against FERTS." His eyes narrowed. "A threat like your rogue companions, for instance." He stepped forward, closing his hands around 201's throat. "Or a threat like you. I think I'm going to enjoy this, 201," he said.

201 gasped, struggling for air.

The sound of Pinnacle Officer Wilcox's laughter echoed through her head. She could feel him now, infiltrating her thoughts as her essence weakened. She struggled against Morton's grip, trying to block the voice from her mind but her efforts were futile.

I shall take great pleasure in watching Morton expire you, 201. How fitting, don't you agree? You have been nothing but a nuisance from the beginning, a mere diversion in the evolution of this great facility. Do not think that you were anything greater than this. Do not think that you were anything other than just another ordinary Internee.

Morton squeezed his hands tighter, eyes becoming animated at the clipped choking sounds escaping from 201's throat. 201's eyes widened, fear crossing her features. Pinnacle Officer Wilcox sighed, the sound caressing the blood rushing at her temples.

There. That is the look I like. Fear looks good on you.

Morton smiled down on 201's flushed face, the whiteness of her eyes standing out against the unnatural shade of red. He released his grip slightly, adjusting his hold.

"Perhaps now you will find out the meaning of true gratitude. Say the Requital and I shall make this quick. Come on now, we are gathered here to give thanks..." He released his hold on 201, allowing her to speak.

201 gasped, coughing. She wheezed, sucking in as much air as she could manage as she raised her eyes to Officer Morton. "Never." She coughed once more. "You are a coward. A lackey, isn't that what Cerberus calls you?" She sucked in air, breath rattling. "No, you didn't know. And now you have been promoted to guard Officer and you are still a lackey. No amount of insignia will change that. You are as expendable as the rest of us."

"Shut your mouth!" The slap stung her cheek but she raised her head once more, smiling at Officer Morton as the siren continued to sound out through the grounds below.

"They will come for you," said 201. "I will come for you. After I am expired, my last hope is that you never sleep. I shall visit you in your dreams until you are driven senseless..." 201 hit the ground, face stinging from another blow. She squeezed her eyes against the pain and gritted her teeth, cheek pressed against the stone floor. Rough hands pulled her to her knees and she heard the sound of trousers unfastening.

"You talk too much, defective. You will show your gratitude in another way. You may be a defective but you still have one use left." His trousers dropped to the floor as he yanked 201's head towards him. 201 scrabbled backwards on her heels, pulling away but Officer Morton kept her head steady, his large hand propelling her forward. 201 cried out in protest. Not again, she thought. Please no, not again.

"You are far too tense, this won't do. I guess will have to use your mouth instead. Open up for me now, if you don't I will make you will wish you had."

Officer Jorg's voice drifted through her mind. She squeezed her eyes tight, trying to resist the force of Morton's hands clamping around her jaw.

Her mind flew to the forest. She was with Rafaella and Caltha, fighting alongside her companions, bastard sword held high. The images flooded her mind, flashing and flickering behind her eyelids. A crash sounded against the stone floor but she found she could not open her eyes. The siren throbbed, the rhythmic drone pulsing through her consciousness.

"Do not make me say it again."

Officer Jorg's voice filled her senses, bile rising in her throat. She blocked out the feel of his rough hand, the spattering of wetness as it trickled across her face, flowing, cascading in rivulets, the sickly taste of blood as she bit her lip.

Officer Morton's grip tightened around her throat one last time and her vision greyed at the edges. The air sucked from her body as her surroundings faded, became blurry, and went black.

Everything was quiet.

A figure was glowing before her, tall, graceful, the essence of the figure outlined in a vibrant green. The figure grew brighter as it took shape, solidifying and strengthening as 201 watched, her mouth falling open. A flash of brilliance filled her vision and 201 shielded her eyes from the glare. The luminescence emanating from Beth #1, the first Beth, was too much to take in at once. 201 could sense her, her face was beautiful, kind. She felt a sense of compassion wash through her. 201 could feel Beth looking upon her with sadness, but also a sense of welcoming, of acceptance.

So, 201, you have come to me. I have been waiting for you.

"I cannot look at you, there is too much light..."

I have grown strong, 201. You and your companions, your communion with the wise ones, it has all helped me to become stronger. Stronger against Wilcox. For that I thank you.

"I am sorry, Beth. I tried to stop Morton but he was too strong. I couldn't save them. I have failed."

You have not failed, 201. Far from it. You are a brave fighter, and your heart is strong. You care for others, this is your strength. But this can also be your weakness, if you let it. It can destroy you as well as save you.

"It's too late. They will be helpless against the beacon. The Epsilon Fighters are too strong now, it will end my companions. It all ends here, today. I will not see it, unfortunately."

Come, 201. Come closer so I can see you better.

201 stepped forward into Beth's embrace. Beth welcomed her with a sigh, arms outstretched.

You are correct about one thing, 201. It all ends here. Today. It all ends here. 201, look at me.

"I can't. You have grown too bright. My eyes..."

Beth gripped her arm, long fingernails digging in to her skin, leaving marks as they went.

Concentrate, 201. You cannot see, even though the answer lies before you.

201 tried to pull away but the fingernails gripped harder.

"Beth... you're hurting me..."

Open your eyes, 201. Open your eyes and see.

"I don't understand... I cannot open them. I cannot see. It is too bright, there is too much light..."

Beth's voice raised in volume, filling 201's ears and blocking out her thoughts. Her voice became higher in pitch, ragged and raspy. The fingernails began to draw blood, deep scratches etched into the skin of her arms. Her vision began to blur at the edges and the light seeping through the corners of her eyes had begun to fade, becoming colder, enveloping her in darkness.

Open your eyes, 201.
See, 201.
See.

See, 201.
Now you can see.
Everything went black.

44

The beacon blared, the siren echoing through the trees at the edge of the suspension zone. In the glow of the artificial lights seeping from FERTS, the warriors from the camp pushed back against the growing tide of Epsilon Fighters and Internees, fending off blows from spathas, tridents and bastard swords. Rafaella swung her saber, knocking an Internee to the ground as she caught sight of 263 charging towards her, dressed in red, eyes dark and full of emptiness. Rafaella raised her hands towards 263.

"Wait, 263! Stop! Think about what you're doing." Rafaella took a step back, conscious of 263's changed demeanor.

263 hesitated, momentarily confused. She glanced around, unsure of her surroundings.

Rafaella put her hands out, palms facing open. "263, just stop. Think of what 201 fought for. What we all fight for. You can be free. You know that now. Why are you fighting us? We can fight against this together, whatever this is."

The siren punctuated her words, rhythmically blaring its steady tattoo, the sounds washing over the fallen bodies of the opposing forces. 263 looked up, locking eyes with Rafaella. Rafaella watched as a pained look washed over 263's face. The look faded from her eyes as another expression darkened her features. 263's lips curled upwards into a smile, eyes narrowing, teeth bared.

"263?" Rafaella whispered. The sounds of the battle raged around them, the sound of metal on metal assaulting their senses. The sickening sounds of metal against flesh sounded as Fighters fell, their cries reaching to the sky.

263 advanced on Rafaella, raising the points of her trident. "We are gathered here to give thanks…" 263 jabbed, grinning widely, her trident colliding with Rafaella's saber. 263 lunged, her eyes flat and lifeless, as Rafaella blocked the attack. She stepped back, eyes scanning her surroundings, fixing her gaze on Rafaella.

"…to Pinnacle Officer Cerberus and FERTS!" 263 roared, charging towards Rafaella. Rafaella dodged to the side, bringing an elbow to 263's face, the momentum knocking herself, 263 and her saber to the ground. 263 launched herself up from the ground and smiled, eyes blank, teeth coated with blood, a low chuckle bursting forth from her lips.

She loomed above Rafaella, her eyes devoid of emotion. Rafaella knelt, reaching out, feeling for her saber, the blade just out of reach. 263 ground her heel against the handle, locking eyes with Rafaella as she raised her trident.

Caltha fended off another blow from an Epsilon Internee, knocking her out of the way. She twisted to the side, turning her head to find Rafaella on her knees, 263's trident descending in an arc towards her head.

"Raf! No!"

45

Everything was dark. 201 felt a slick wetness on her face. Afraid to open her eyes, she tried to suck in a breath, the pain shooting through her throat. She hacked out a breath, coughing and wheezing. Her eyes would not open of their own accord. She tried to force them but the sting seeping in halted her progress.

201 felt the pressure on her throat and jaw lessen to a limp caress. She forced her eyes open once more, blinking, her vision flooding with red, the sting jarring her eyes as she blinked and squeezed her eyes open and shut, then open again to clear her vision. The hand slid away, slicked with moisture, the silence in the control room heavy, thickening the air.

She opened her eyes to the sting, blinking her eyes open and closing them again, yet still she could not see. She raised a hand to her face. It was too warm, slippery and hot, the unmistakable metallic tang seeping through her pores and flooding her nostrils. She wiped at her brow, catching the drips as they fell, forcing her smarting eyes open to see Officer Morton standing tall, towering above her, blood gushing forth from the base of his neck, his upturned head rocking back and forth, scratching rhythmically against the stone floor. His legs buckled underneath him, body tilting to the side and crashing to the ground to reveal Reno, arm raised, 201's bastard sword in his hand. 201 looked into Reno's eyes and he stared back, his expression blank.

The pool of blood from Officer Morton's body fanned out, edging towards her, expanding to reach her knees. 201 did not move. She studied Reno's face, his eyes meeting her own, widening slightly.

201 lunged at the console, banging her fist down on the button. The steady blare of the beacon ceased. Everything fell quiet. The sounds of breathing in the control room magnified.

"201, wait," said Reno.

201 screamed in frustration, ripping the monitor from its console. She hurled it to the ground, the pieces scattering across the stone floor. She pulled against the panels, cutting her fingers in the process, kicking out with her boot at the remains of the monitor.

"201." 201 turned her head, face bloodied and eyes narrowed to meet Reno's face. "Stop, 201. You will hurt yourself."

"Done now. It's done now." 201 smiled, eyes bright against the darkness of the blood masking her face. She sat back on her heels and laughed, a gentle sound bubbling up from deep within her. She held her stomach as she laughed harder, breathy huffs escaping her lips as she kept her eyes on the control room door, watching for signs of movement. Reno had not moved from his spot, impassive features giving away nothing.

"Thank you," she whispered.

Reno smiled back, a small chuckle escaping from his lips. "I told you to wait before coming here."

"The others couldn't wait, Reno." 201 swiped her face, smearing blood and ash. "Raf and Cal couldn't wait."

Reno nodded. He looked down at the form of Officer Morton, face becoming grim.

"Do not regret this, Reno. I certainly do not. We must destroy everything." 201 exhaled sharply. "Another could press this button. Another could become Pinnacle Officer. We must destroy it all. There is no time to waste."

"You." Reno cast his eyes towards Operator Linum, still huddled against the corner of the control room. Linum looked over at Reno and 201, surprised that Reno had remembered he was there at all. "Do we have a problem here?"

"No." Operator Linum shook his head, his hair plastered to his face with sweat.

"Well come on, then. Help me take this thing apart."

"Wait!" Linum stopped Reno before he could reach the console. Reno tensed, ready to defend himself against the Operator.

"You need to do this first." He looked over at 201, shaking his head. "You are indeed lucky to not be expired after that." He glanced around at the shards of the broken monitor. Reno stood still, waiting for

Operator Linum to move. Operator Linum edged past Reno and 201, hands raised in a placating gesture.

"I have no wish to harm you. Please." He made his way to the console, bending down to inspect the apparatus.

Linum rummaged around behind the console, flicking a switch and unplugging the long black electrical cord from the wall and stepping back as 201 and Reno began to dismantle the controls.

46

Caltha edged back, faking to the side as she knocked another Epsilon Internee to the ground.

"Raf! Look out!" Raf caught her eye, signaling Caltha with a slight nod of her head. 263 laughed, bringing her trident down towards Rafaella's head. Rafaella kicked her foot at 263's knee, rolling out of the path of the sharpened points. 263 buckled, hitting the dirt with a cry, trident wobbling from her grasp and thumping to the ground, points embedded in the soil. She pulled herself to her feet, eyes trained on Rafaella.

The cold blade of Caltha's bone dagger rested against 263's neck as she struggled to stay upright. The tip stayed firm at her throat, pushing firmly without breaking the skin.

"That's enough, 263. Don't get any closer," Caltha said, leaning close to her ear.

"We are gathered to give thanks..." 263 struggled against Caltha's hold. The blade remained firm but Caltha loosened her hold so as not to cut too deeply.

"Stop that. You know it is a lie," said Caltha.

263 reached for her trident. Caltha pushed the blade against her skin, drawing droplets of blood.

"Don't, 263. Come on, I don't want to hurt you. Please."

Rafaella stood before her, holding the point of her saber at 263's chest. "Listen to Cal, 263. You don't have to do this. We can help you," Rafaella said. "What have they done to you?"

263 glanced at Rafaella, grimacing as the siren throbbed at her ears. Her eyes cleared for a brief moment. She looked smaller, less dangerous somehow. The siren blared again. Her body tensed. She shook, fists clenching and unclenching. "I can't... I can't stop it Raf. It won't let me."

Rafaella dodged an incoming blade, a flash of red appearing in her vision as the Epsilon Internee tumbled to the side, slowed by a swift blow from Rafaella's fist. "Fight it, 263! You have to fight it!" The siren droned on as Rafaella turned to find another group of Internees advancing closer in a unified sea of red, followed by blue, orange and white.

The siren continued, assaulting their ears as they edged back towards the perimeter. Caltha dragged 263, kicking and snarling as they made their way back towards the tree line.

"No no no! It will expire me! The beacon!"

"Then tell them to stop." Rafaella's voice was calm, her mouth pressed against 263's ear. "Tell them to stay back. I'm not joking with you."

"They will never stop until FERTS is secured! I will never stop until I have earned the thanks and veneration of FERTS!" She squeezed her eyes shut, fighting for control. Her next words sounded less rigid, more like herself. "I'm warning you, Raf. You all need to run. They will not rest until you are all expired!"

The siren halted mid-signal.

263 kicked out from Caltha's grip, dropping to the ground, panting.

The advancing Internees from Epsilon, Kappa, Beta and Omega paused, weapons clutched in hand, glancing around at their surroundings, blinking.

Rafaella looked down at 263, scowling and raising her saber in warning.

"Wait, wait! Don't hurt me, Raf. I'm okay." She looked over at the gathering of Internees spread out before her on the grounds of FERTS. "Don't hurt us. We're okay."

47

Games Operator Farrenlowe sat in his office, scraps of paper with Epsilon Fighter names lay strewn about the table, ready for the next 'random' drawing. He and his fellow games attendants knew perfectly well that the names were chosen well before the drawing. The Beta Internee would carry the name in her sleeve, 'drawing' it at random at the appropriate time in the proceedings. Sometimes there would only be one name in the bucket. The Beta Internees never questioned the decision. It was the will of the Pinnacle Officer for each Fighter to be chosen as such, and no discussion was to be had in the matter. The wheel needed a good oiling as well, he thought. Oil was scarce at this time of year, yet the stores would hold out until they could replenish the supply. In addition to this, the notch at the back of the Epsilon wheel had begun to stick, affecting the rate of slowing during the spin presentation.

The next 'random' Fighter was marked down for selection. The wheel would be set for spatha, her weapon of choice. It was imperative that the Epsilon Fighters be led to believe that they were truly lucky and that the wheel was assisting them in some way. It was necessary to maintain the overall mood of the occasion. It mattered not, regardless of the chosen Fighter's weapon. They would be no match for the seasoned Fighters. But it was important for the Epsilon Fighters to feel they had a chance, that perhaps fortune was with them as they entered the ring. It made for a greater spectacle, in any case. The Officers enjoyed a good slaughter, and Games Operator Farrenlowe was more than pleased to deliver it to them.

Games Operator Farrenlowe smiled to himself. He was beginning to warm to the new Pinnacle Officer's amendments. Tonight he would choose the week's new addition to Beta Circuit, just 15Y, as of today. The new standard for Vassal selection was at a more appropriate level, and in his opinion, a prudent choice. Why choose Vassals so late in their development? Surely they would be over limit before long, a waste of good Vassal stock. The addition of the 15Ys and up would better utilize the available Internee pool. Farrenlowe preferred them younger, in any case.

He leaned back in his seat. Yes, he would choose the new Beta recruit this night, and the following nights, after the monthly Epsilon Games, he would celebrate with another...

The sound of boots on stone filtered up the hall. The steps clattered, haphazardly, unlike the ordered strides of the usual Officers. A cry sounded from the top of the stairs, a muffled choke reverberating throughout the hallway. The sound was deep, guttural. The sound of an Officer...

The footsteps gathered momentum, scrabbling, clattering, the clink of weapons heavy in the halls.

Something was wrong.

The door banged open to reveal a horde of Epsilon Fighters, fully armed with spathas, tridents, bastard swords and scimitars. Games Operator Farrenlowe held still, careful not to betray the shock of fear that ran down the length of his body.

Surely they wouldn't dare...

"Beloved Fighters of Epsilon." His voice was flat, without intonation. "It appears you have been dealing with this disturbance and have returned victorious. This is indeed great news."

"It is, Games Operator Farrenlowe. Our Fighters are truly lucky," said 263. Games Operator Farrenlowe relaxed visibly, shuffling the papers on his desk.

"FERTS thanks you. You have earned the veneration of Epsilon Circuit, and of the Officers. Pinnacle Officer Cerberus will be proud."

One of the Epsilon Fighters chuckled, earning an elbow in the ribs from 263.

"And for that we are truly grateful, is that not correct, fellow Fighters?" Murmurs and affirmations of approval resounded throughout the group. "But I did not disclose the true nature of our victory."

"What do you mean?" Games Operator Farrenlowe's hand paused at the drawer of his desk, hovering over its contents.

"Why, our victory against the Officers, Games Operator Farrenlowe. Our shared victory with the rogues. We no longer fight for you, or FERTS, or the glory of Epsilon."

"That is preposterous!" Games Operator Farrenlowe banged his fist on the desk with one hand, a distracting move, reaching down with the other to snatch the knife from his drawer.

"What can be more gratifying than the glory of Epsilon?" he asked, sliding the knife into his palm. The Internees were closer now, edging towards the desk to surround Games Operator Farrenlowe.

"Why, that is simple, Games Operator Farrenlowe. Our freedom."

Games Operator Farrenlowe turned to 263, pointing the knife towards her. The Fighters were close now, too close. He thrust the knife at 263, glancing her arm. 263 knocked it away with her spatha.

"Guard Officer! Guard Officer!" Games Operator Farrenlowe's voice was shrill, echoing against the stone walls.

263's face was somber, a frown crossing her face.

"They can't hear you."

Farrenlowe screamed as the Internees closed the final distance between them. His scream stopped when the spatha pierced his chest, a cold pain shooting through his heart.

He lay on the floor by the desk, staring into the eyes of 263, the spatha still protruding from his chest.

"You will be sent to Zeta Circuit for your treason," he murmured. "Your punishment will be my comfort." A hint of a smile crept to his lips.

263 placed her foot on Farrenlowe's chest, resting her hand on the hilt of the spatha.

"There will be no Zeta Circuit after this day," said 263. Farrenlowe's eyes widened as he spluttered, a sheen of blood coating his lips. "We have seen it, *all* of the Internees have seen it. The bones, the pit. Our companions piled like waste. Our Fighters, stacked against each other. This is how you venerate us." Farrenlowe coughed, spittle and blood coating his cheeks. "But do not worry, Farrenlowe. We shall honor you with the same veneration afforded to our fellow Internees." With that she pressed her foot down, pulling the blade from his chest, watching his flushed, shiny face begin to pale as the life drained from his body.

The tinny crackle of a radio sounded in the hallway. 263 charged through the doors, followed closely by the rest of the Epsilon Fighters.

The young Officers stood before them, eyes wide. The first Officer raised his hands above his head. The second stared at the floor, face pale, a tear escaping from his eye.

"I do not wish to be expired," said the first. "We have no wish to fight you." The second Officer stared at the stone floor, hands shaking as he clasped them together.

"Expire them!" called one of the Epsilon Fighters, raising her trident.

"No, please," said the first Officer, as the second whimpered.

"Wait." 263 raised her hand to stop the Fighters from advancing. "Did you not hear him? They do not wish to fight us," she said.

"They are Officers, 263. All Officers must be expired." The Epsilon Fighters edged forward, the two Officers shrinking back.

"No, that was not the plan. It cannot be this way. If we expire them all, without thought, we are no better than what we fight." She stepped towards the first Officer.

"You were ordered here?" The first Officer nodded. "Where are the ones who sent you?" The first Officer clicked his radio off and handed it to 263. He let out a shaky breath. "There are three of them. They guard the entrance to Beta Circuit. One of them stands watch above the walkway. We did not wish to come here."

"What is your name, Officer?"

"Sylan. And this is Ganne."

"Do you know of Zeta Circuit?" The Officers shook their heads. 263 studied their faces for a time.

"Well, Sylan and Ganne. We have decided to let you go free. I suggest the entrance on the North side. Keep your hands up, just in case."

"What?" exclaimed another Epsilon Fighter, stepping forward. "Are you senseless? They will rejoin the other Officers." She waved her hands in the air. "They will warn them!"

263 studied the faces of the Officers once more. "No, I do not believe they will do that. I believe Sylan and Ganne here want this to be over, just as we do."

"We will not rejoin the Officers. We wish to leave. Return to school."

"I believe you. But if we let you go, you will not return to your school, not yet. I have a task for you. I ask that you travel to the townships and let it be known that FERTS is no more. You may tell them that the Internees are free and the Vassals in the townships are to be released. We will have eyes on the townships, and we will be watching. You may also tell them that should anyone wish to challenge us, we will be ready." An enthusiastic cheer raised up from the Epsilon Fighters.

"But what is important is this. Hundreds from Zeta Circuit, hundreds like us have been burned, expired, piled in a pit in the forest. We now know what our fate would have been, whether it be from Beta, Omega, Epsilon or Kappa. We were all to be expired at some stage, that was the Pinnacle Officer's command. We have seen it. We know now where this would have ended, for all of us."

Sylan shook his head. "It can't be..."

"That is not all. Should any wish to continue on the Pinnacle Officer's 'work', they will join our fallen companions in the pit. Is that clear?"

Sylan nodded once more, leading Ganne away, arm around his shoulder.

263 and the rest of the Epsilon Fighters filed out down the hallway, heading for Beta Circuit.

48

201 leaned on Reno's shoulder as he pushed them through the heavy doors and into the coolness of the evening, the moon bathing them with light.

Rafaella looked up from attending to the wounded from both sides to see 201, covered head to knees in blood, her familiar hazel eyes peeking out from the mask of red.

"201!" Rafaella rushed to 201, taking her arm. "Are you okay? Are you hurt?"

201 smiled at Rafaella, squinting at her, wiping the blood from her eyes.

"I am. I'm okay." 201 grinned, her eyes scanning the few remaining injured Fighters. "We are all scarred. But unbroken, after all."

"Yeah... okay." Rafaella helped her down to the ground. "You look like you're about to fall down. Come on."

"She'll be fine," Reno said.

"Yeah? You'd better hope so," muttered Rafaella. 201 tugged on her sleeve.

"Raf, Raf," 201 said, her voice croaking. "He expired Officer Morton. Stopped him from..."

"Stopped him from what?"

201 wiped her mouth, shaking her head. Reno shot a warning look at Rafaella.

"I'm not finished with you, Reno. You're going to explain all of this to me. At length."

"I look forward to it," Reno called after her, watching Rafaella as she headed towards the pile of supply packs. A faint smile crossed Reno's features.

"What are you smiling about?" 201 asked him as he bent to check on her.

"Nothing."

"I hardly ever see you smile, Reno. This is good." 201 winced as she lay back on the ground, a supply pack behind her head.

"Perhaps I have not had much to smile about."

"I know what you mean," she murmured, drifting as her eyes became heavy. "I am glad. We did it."

Reno sat beside her, watching over the rest of the Fighters as 201 fell into a shallow sleep. "Yes, we did," he whispered.

201 opened her eyes from sleep. Gritty with dried blood, she grimaced as her eyelashes stuck together, straining to open. The moon was lower in the sky, the sounds of bustling activity surrounding her. She ran a hand over her face, groaning as she attempted to sit up, propping herself on one elbow.

"Sleep well?"

Rafaella's voice drifted down from above her. She caught a glimpse of Rafaella's boots.

"Mmph. I can't remember."

"Yeah, well you were out for a while. Thought we'd let you sleep for a bit."

The door to FERTS opened. Rafaella gripped 201's arm, giving it a shake.

"201," she whispered. "Look."

201 sat upright, using Rafaella's knee for leverage. The doors were wedged open, a rock placed against each side. The Epsilon Fighters filed out, still clasping their weapons, the red of their regulation jumpsuits soaked wet in patches.

Blood. Red on red. That's why it doesn't show.

The red jumpsuits continued to emerge from the shadow of the doorway, faces squinting as the artificial light bathed their faces. White, then blue jumpsuits began to peek out from the gathering of red, the bemused faces of the Beta and Omega Internees shielding their eyes through the glare, trying to comprehend the scattered weapons in the darkness, the bloodied ground and the warriors from the camp tending to the wounded.

Soon came the swarm or orange. The Kappa Internees, still carrying their axes, stepped through the doorway, their jumpsuits soaked in sweat.

201's eyes filled with tears.

"I have always wanted to see this," she said.

"Me too." Rafaella's voice cracked on the last word.

"Raf? Are you... crying?"

"Yeah, maybe. But you never saw me, so just remember... oh..."

A crowd of Zeta Internees shuffled out, the first group emerging from their hiding place, stopping to peer out into the grounds, the group behind bumping into their backs.

"So many of them, Raf," 201 whispered, watching as the Zeta Internees filed out. One Internee helped another through the doorway, blinking up at the moonlight. The first turned to the other and smiled, nudging her and pointing to the trees, the grass, the moon in the sky. They grinned as they made their way past 201 towards the tree line.

The Zeta Internees made their way into the grounds, their dirty jumpsuits hanging from their shapeless frames. Some shuffled, some were carried by their fellow Internees. One Internee leaned against the front of the facility, sliding down to the ground, exhausted. Jotha ran to help her up, leading her away to a patch of grass by the trees.

"Look at them, Raf. I forgot how small they are..."

One Zeta Internee turned to stare at 201 and Rafaella. She raised a bony hand, giving a feeble wave. Her mouth turned up at the edges. It was a strange look, but one she recognized well.

The face of someone who has forgotten how to smile.

Rafaella wrapped her arms around 201, patting her back.

"You did good today, 201. I'm proud of you."

"Thanks Raf," 201 whispered, stray tears soaking into Rafaella's tunic.

Rafaella pulled back, trying to wipe the blood away from 201's face. "You need to clean off your face, though. You look kind of frightening."

"You're right," 201 said, feeling the grainy texture of the dried blood. "I almost forgot. I'll do it now. I don't want to frighten them any more than necessary." She gestured to the Zeta Internees.

"From what I've heard, it would take more than that to scare them," Rafaella said.

Jotha and Petra rushed to the Zeta Internees, handing out water. One Zeta Internee clutched a little one, who appeared to be asleep for the time being. The little one appeared weak, taking shallow breaths. Petra handed her a blanket, wrapping the little one in another layer for warmth.

"Hey," said Caltha, putting a hand on Rafaella's shoulder.

"Hey, Cal," said Rafaella, pulling her into an embrace. "You holding together okay?"

"You asked me that three times today. Yes, I'm fine."

201 stood beside them, wiping the blood from her face. "You saved them. Both of you, all of you. I don't know how to thank you."

"Couldn't have done it without you. Anyway, this is what we do," Rafaella said.

201 watched the Internees helping each other to the ground, gathering blankets and supplies. "I used to be like them, Raf. I was them. Perhaps part of me will always be like that."

"201, Cal and I have lived free for many years. We're not the only ones who deserve this." She gave 201's arm a squeeze. "We all do."

49

A number of days passed. Rafaella, Caltha and scores of Internees stripped FERTS of its equipment, its power source and its ration resources. Piles of parts, wires, various gadgets and decorative fabrics lay in piles on the ground, covered and ready for the many journeys they would need to transport their bounty. Many of the items would be traded for animals and food, as they had no use for decorative flourishes. The survivors had dined on Officer's rations both nights, and morale was high within their new, much larger group.

201 stood before FERTS, the lettering staring back at her from the entrance. She glanced back to the Zeta Internees, the blue jumpsuits of Omega, the white of Beta, the red of Kappa, the faces of the Epsilon Fighters glaring back at the facility. 201 turned back to the structure, eyes scanning upwards.

"Burn it," 201 said.

Petra glanced at the building, then back to 201. "Have you lost your mind? It's made of stone. I don't know if you know about these things, but stone doesn't burn."

"No," 201 said, tapping the outer wall. "It is not only made of stone. There is wood in there, and it will burn."

"201 is right," said Kap. "I have taken a look, a cursory inspection of the structure. The stone is held together by wooden beams, mortar in the joins. It will burn. Perhaps not fully but..."

"Even so, why..."

"Because we need to," said 201. "They need to." She said, motioning to the Internees behind her. "We all need to."

"Is that what everyone wants?" Rafaella asked. "If so, I say we go with 201's idea." Petra, Rafaella and Kap looked to 201. 201 strode towards a large rock, climbing to the top and standing above the Internees. She stood before the scattered Internees, the field awash with reds, blues, whites and greys. Some noticed her presence, gathering closer. Others spoke amongst themselves in hushed tones.

"Former Internees of FERTS!" 201 called, standing atop the large rock, adjusting her footing so as not to tumble off. The field of Internees turned their heads in the direction of her voice.

"I need to know what you think. Soon, we will leave this place. Do we leave the facility as it stands?"

"No, I cannot look at it!" called a voice from the crowd.

"What else can we do? Leave it! I wish to be far from here!" another cried out. The voices came from all sides, blending into a discordant drone. 201 raised her hands, palms facing outward.

"Stop! I cannot hear you all at once. We must..." 201 looked around her spot atop the rock, scratching her neck. She needed some way to decide this in certainty. She thought back to the way Rafaella and Caltha consulted Petra, Jotha and the others. Perhaps this would work here. It was worth a try, at least. She looked back at the crowd.

"I want you to raise your hand if you agree, but you need to keep your hand down if you disagree with what I say." There were murmurs from the sea of Internees, the voices muttering in confusion.

"Do we leave FERTS as it stands?" A mass of hands raised in the air. 201 looked around at the number of hands, memorizing the size of each of the sections.

"Or do we burn it?" A similar number of hands raised in the air. 201 was confused. Could it be that the opinions of the former FERTS Internees was so evenly spread? There must have been a mistake made along the way. Something did not feel right, she had done something wrong, a crucial step. 201 stood motionless, scanning the crowd and the still-raised hands. Perhaps this was not the best system with which to decide. She pondered for a moment, the realization clearing in her mind.

The ones who said yes to the first idea did not think they could say yes again. And with the second idea introduced, perhaps none would have said yes to the first idea if they knew what the second idea entailed. There must be another phrasing, another way of asking the questions. It is the only way for each to decide for themselves after knowing the two options.

"I will ask again, just to be sure. There are two choices. Now that you know the choices, keep this in mind when you raise your hand."

"Do we leave FERTS as it stands?" She looked over the crowd, scanning the number of hands. There were only a few hands in the air.

"Or do we burn it?" The hands seemed to move as one. Some stood on their toes, outstretched arms shooting into the air and reaching to the sky.

"Burn it," said one.

"Burn it!" said another.

201 stepped off the rock, passing Kap and Rafaella. "I guess we are burning it, then."

"You heard 201, let's get to it," Rafaella said.

The Kappa Internees grouped together as one, heading for one of the doors and filing through in formation.

Petra stared after them. "I don't understand. Where are they going?"

"They know where the wood is kept," 201 said, watching them file through the door.

The Kappa Internees piled the wood through the halls, leaving a trail of wooden shavings as they went. They stacked wood in the largest rooms, layering the wood and connecting the trails with yet more of the wood shavings. Hours passed, the remaining stronger Internees of Zeta, the Epsilon Fighters and even some of the Omega and Beta Internees joined in, working in harmony to build the trail.

When they had finished, night was almost upon them. The sun was low in the sky, a red and orange hue lighting up the side of the facility. Rafaella bent down, flint in hand. She began to scratch the flint.

Stop this, 201. You must see. Open your eyes and see.

The trail of moss and wood shavings near the entrance began to smolder. The voice rose once more in 201's head, visions of bright light, blinding her, almost toppling her off-balance.

Find me, said the voice. See, 201. See.

201 steadied herself, an image of blue eyes blinked back at her when she closed her eyes.

Beth?

201's eyes flicked open to see Rafaella leaning over a small flame, the glow spreading to illuminate her face. "Wait! Not yet! Not yet!" 201 ran towards the doorway, clearing the smoking pile of kindling and rushing through the hallways, dodging logs and shavings as she weaved around the debris.

"What the..." Rafaella stomped on the smoldering heap, watching the figure of 201 retreating back into the hallways of FERTS.

201 ran, Rafaella's curses following her as she went. She ran, guided by the thought of blue eyes, staring back at her, filling her vision. The words made their way back into her mind, the voice in her head clearer this time, louder than before.

Find me, 201.

201 burst through the door to Pinnacle Officer Cerberus' office, rushing past his desk, past his loose

papers and the quartz paperweight securing the pile. She stood before the jar, the eyes from her dream staring back at her. She reached out to it, touching the edges.

The jar sat on the shelf, the rusty tinge of the liquid swirling from side to side. The blue eyes settled in the liquid, spinning in opposite directions until they came to a stop, facing her. The label was precise, in Pinnacle Officer Wilcox's writing. Beth. #1. 26Y.

No!

Wilcox's voice was faint, echoing in the back of her mind. The hint of a smile crept in at the corners of her mouth.

No! Not Beth! No!

She clamped her hands around the jar, ensuring her grip was tight. She strode out, securing the jar in her hands, heading back down the hallway as fast as she could walk.

She emerged from the doorway into the semi-darkness of the evening. The sun was almost beyond the horizon, the field around them bathed in pink. Rafaella stood near the entrance, flint in one hand, kindling in the other. She scowled at 201 as she emerged from the entrance of FERTS for the last time.

"Damn it, 201! What..." Rafaella looked at the jar and back to 201.

201 nodded in deference, making her way past Rafaella, hands clamped tightly around the jar. "Now you can burn it," she said as she made her way to the

edge of the tree line, settling herself underneath one of the trees.

Rafaella muttered something unintelligible, kneeling down on one knee to scratch the flint. After a moment, the kindling began to smolder. The Internees gathered around in wonder, watching the first licks of flame curl up from the pile. Rafaella dropped another load of kindling on the pile, walking away from the entrance. "You might want to all get back near the tree line," she said, ushering the group away from the growing flames.

Some of the Internees filed out towards the trees. Others stayed to watch. Rafaella doubled back, standing between them and the flames expanding around the doorway. "Now. Now's a good time to get back, come on." The Internees backed away, moving towards the tree line.

The frame of the doorway caught alight, the flames flickering around the FERTS lettering above the entrance before catching on the beams above. Gasps and soft cries filled the air.

201 sucked in a breath, leaning back against the tree. The light from the fire danced across her face. She turned the jar, slowly inching it around until Beth's eyes faced the flames. "See?" she whispered to the jar. "Do you see this now?" The eyes in the jar turned in the liquid to face her. "FERTS is burning," she said. "Watch it as it burns."

A crash sounded within the facility as one of the support beams collapsed, taking the stones along with it. 201 watched the flames spreading along the wood, tears leaking from the corner of her eyes. The lights grew brighter, the jar illuminating in her hand. Flames licked out from the top of the building, clamoring for height as they competed against each other, reaching ever upward to the night sky. The heat radiated outwards to reach the tree line.

201 felt the coolness of the jar in her hand. It would not stay that way for long.

It's time.

She stepped away from the tree, reaching for a shovel. She broke the earth, piling it to the side until she had made a square shaped hole. The flames warmed her back, sweat beading on her arms and forehead. She wiped her brow, neatening the edges of the earth, patting at the dirt until it was firm. She stood back, grasping the jar and holding it to the light.

"I see everything," she whispered to Beth, unfastening the jar. "I understand now." The lid of the jar made a sucking noise, opening with a click. The liquid burned her eyes, her nostrils stinging from the fumes. She turned her face away, coughing and gasping in a breath.

"This is for you, Beth. This is what you deserved when your essence was taken. Now is the time for you to take it back." With that she knelt, coughing as the fumes burned the breath from her body. She poured the liquid in the hole, sending her thoughts to Beth, sending reverence.

The eyes rolled from the jar, resting on the dampened earth within the hole. She grasped the shovel, filling in the dirt. Each pile from the shovel dampened the effect of the fumes but 201 did not rush. Beth deserved more than that. She piled the earth back in the hole, filling it in. She searched around for a stone, lifting it to the head of the flattened earth and placing it securely in the ground.

"Rest now, Beth. You can rest." She collapsed to the ground, leaning against the tree, her brow dotted with sweat.

"I venerate you, we all venerate you. You are free." 201 closed her eyes.

Flames erupted from the top of the facility, another beam collapsing and taking a corner of the building with it to the ground. Rubble lay in piles at the edges of the building, smoke rising to the sky. The flames at the top of the facility roared to life, gathering intensity with each moment. The night sky was illuminated with light, a light that reached out across the suspension zone, brightening the perimeter, the shadows of the trees lengthening, flickering from right to left.

201 edged her way up the trunk of the tree to stand. She felt the rough bark against her tunic, the earth beneath her feet. The flames danced, brightening her surroundings, illuminating the grass, the leaves, the stones of the suspension zone, casting shadows as they changed direction.

Above the facility, a lone figure emerged from the flames. Beth's eyes, bright and blue, stronger now, her essence strengthened, her hair flowing in waves, swirling and stretching out over the facility. She smiled at 201, raising a hand in farewell. She wavered in the heat, shimmering as she faded. Her essence brightened for a moment, then disappeared.

Another form rose from the flames, his bald head shining, his face contorted in pain.

Wilcox.

His scream filled her ears, echoing throughout the perimeter. 201's eyes darted to the side but the Internees were staring at the flames, giving no indication that they could see or hear anything but the flames licking through FERTS.

Pinnacle Officer Wilcox's uniform smoked, insignia falling from his chest one by one and disappearing into the rubble. His face hollowed out, flames engulfing his mouth, his eyes, tendrils of smoke filing the sockets and pouring out, filling the night sky.

"Goodbye, Wilcox," 201 said, watching as the light brightened to a garish red, illuminating the tree line as if in daylight.

Wilcox's scream became louder, the pressure in her ears building. 201 gripped her ears, dropping to her knees.

Pinnacle Officer Wilcox exploded in a burst of brightness. From his chest, flashes of blues, reds, oranges, escaped, tendrils of greys and whites filling the night sky. Faces, insignia, jumpsuits, all flashed from the flames in a swirl of light, unbound, releasing to the sky, making their way towards the distant brightness of the stars.

So many... there are so many...

The voice of Beth rose up around her, swirling through the air as the Internees released to the sky in a shower of brightness.

I am the breeze that blows through the forest near the suspension zone, I am the rocks, the pebbles, the shrubs, the craggy mountains and winding streams. I am the forest, the creatures, the sky, the sliver of the moon at night, the orb when it is full. I am the stars, the blanket, the canopy of life from which we began. I am Beth, and I see everything.

Within the mass of figures, 201 thought for a moment that she caught a glimpse of a familiar face, a face that she thought she would never see again. She looked up, trying to find those familiar features, her knees digging into the dirt.

Her chest clenched as the face of 232 emerged, her freckled visage illuminated by the light of the flames, her mischievous blue eyes twinkling. The Internees swirled around her, illuminating the perimeter in a sea of varying shades, each representing their respective former Circuits of FERTS.

The figure of 232 stood motionless amongst the turmoil. She was no longer dressed in her regulation Epsilon jumpsuit, now standing above FERTS, dressed in the attire of a free warrior. She sported a bright blue tunic to match her piercing eyes, her boots made from sturdy leather. She wore dark tan trousers, her tunic fastened with a woven leather belt. Her spatha sat sheathed at her hip, arms hanging loosely at her sides.

232 tilted her head to 201 and smiled down at her, eyes crinkling at the corners. She stood proud, a free woman.

Do you remember what I said, 201? Someday I believe that we, all of us will be free. You were right 201... you were right.

201 blinked, eyes coming in to focus again on the mass of unfamiliar faces as they released into the sky around the place where 232 had appeared. 201 swiped at her cheek, her hand coming away wet. The last of the Internees burst into the sky, their collective sighs and gasps washing over 201. The Internees, once bound to Pinnacle Officer Wilcox, descended to gather around 201, swirling around her, weeping and sighing in relief.

Thank you, they whispered, sighing and laughing, their voices rising and falling as they swarmed around her. *Now we are free.*

Blue eyes blinked from the sky, staring down on 201. They blinked twice, and were gone.

I'm proud of you, 201. You are no longer bound. Now you are truly free.

The words burst through her mind, a torrent flowing through her head, clear as the waterfalls at Akecheta. The stream came forth unbroken, the last of Wilcox's influence separated from her essence, escaping to the sky. 201 collapsed to the ground, the weight of his cloying hold removed from her mind. Beth's parting words hung in the air.

Do you see? Do you understand? Do you see it now?

201 raised her head. "I see it, Beth," she whispered, watching the flames rise, lights illuminating the sky. "I see it now." Ash rained down, swirling through the air and settling to the ground. The symbol of the wise women glimmered, burning its outline into the sky, a swirl of light expanding outwards.

"I see you."

50

The next morning 201 awoke to find Rafaella standing over her. She looked to her right at the figure of Titan who stirred, rubbing at his eyes.

"So, this is Titan," said Rafaella. "I've heard so much about you."

201 yawned, rolling over to face Titan. "Titan, this is Raf. She is a great leader, perhaps the greatest, but you probably noticed that already. Perhaps she would be a good example for your paper when you present it to your College."

Titan sat up, squinting at Rafaella. "Pleased to meet you, Raf."

Rafaella smiled down at him.

201 furrowed her brow, looking up at Rafaella. "Wait a moment. I never told you about Titan."

"Not when you were awake. 201 talks in her sleep." Rafaella turned to Titan with a smile.

"I have bad dreams. Sometimes." 201 looked at the ground.

"You had bad dreams about me?"

"No, those ones weren't bad." Rafaella chortled, nudging Reno, who had appeared behind her. Reno's face broke into a grin as understanding dawned.

"Thanks Raf," 201 said, rising to her feet and holding her hand out to Titan. "That's enough talking." She led Titan towards the cart to load it up with supplies. "That was Raf. She talks a lot. Too much." She shot Rafaella a look as Rafaella settled herself back on a log beside Reno, laughing and shaking her head.

"She's formidable," Titan said, casting a glance in Rafaella's direction. "It's good to be here, 201. I didn't know if I'd see you again."

201 huffed out a breath, securing the load in the cart. "You nearly didn't." 201 pushed a wayward strand of hair behind her ear. She looked up to see Rafaella standing on the highest part of the log. She whistled, signaling to everyone present that it was time to leave.

Rafaella and Caltha loaded up the last cart with supplies salvaged from FERTS. 201 stepped closer to Rafaella, observing the sacks of soybeans filling the cart. 201 wrinkled her nose.

"Don't worry, 201. I'm sure Lina can come up with something more interesting than regulation protein. She can be very creative when it comes to food."

"I hope so," 201 said.

"Are we ready?" Rafaella looked out over the sea of Internees, the jumpsuits lining the path.

Murmurs came from the Internees and they set out, urging the horses forward. They brought with them the Vassal carts from FERTS with Reno at the helm, along with the remaining horses.

Those who could walk, walked. Those who could not were laid out on the carts, eyes trained to the bright blue of the morning sky. Some helped their companions, arms slung around shoulders. 201 walked alongside a Zeta Internee, one arm supporting her weight. Titan stood on the other side, his arm slung around the Internee's waist. He peeked over at 201, giving her a grin. 201 grinned back as they followed the path through the suspension zone on their long journey back to the camp. Back to their companions, back to Lina, Adira and 301. Back to Akecheta. Back...

Home.

Other books in this series:

FERTS
The Rogue Thread
Alpha Field

Other books by this author:

Demon Veil
Open Doors

Sign up to the Grace Hudson newsletter:
www.gracehudson.net

Twitter: @gracehudsonau

Facebook: www.facebook.com/gracehudsonauthor

Goodreads: www.goodreads.com/gracehudson

Manufactured by Amazon.ca
Bolton, ON

18485066R00166